𝓜AUI ISN'T ALWAYS the safe paradise it's made out to be. When ancient island superstitions threaten to rob the Monroe family yet again, they must all find a way to turn fate in a favorable direction. Into the Blue, the third book in the By the Sea series, takes you on an emotional journey filled with hope for a happily ever after.

Jules is the matriarch and center of the Monroe family, having led a healthy and fulfilling life and made something of herself from nothing. Now in her late fifties, she juggles her charity mission, fulfills needs of the family business, provides childcare for her grandchildren, and continues being the best wife she can be to Noah. But everything comes to an abrupt stop when her body says enough, and her mind would rather retreat to a safer place than the one she has carved out in her lifelong attempt to keep her own needs and emotions under lock and key.

Jonah Monroe is Jules' and Noah's eldest child and only son. Despite his not-so-long-ago tour of duty with the service that should've changed his outlook, a childhood tragedy molded him into a reserved man with low self-esteem and a reluctance to rely on others. His past included things he wasn't proud of and might never shed. When he has another chance to be the hero he's always wanted to be, will he accept the kindness of strangers to get him there or will his demons force him to retreat and lose confidence in his own gut feeling and abilities?

Into the Blue

Books by Kay Bratt

You can find them in Kindle Unlimited, too.

BY THE SEA TRILOGY
True to Me
No Place too Far
Into the Blue

THE TALES OF THE SCAVENGER'S DAUGHTERS SERIES
The Palest Ink
The Scavenger's Daughters
Tangled Vines
Bitter Winds
Red Skies

LIFE OF WILLOW DUOLOGY
Somewhere Beautiful
Where I Belong

SWORN SISTERS DUOLOGY
A Welcome Misfortune
To Move the World

STANDALONE NOVELS
Wish Me Home
Dancing with the Sun
Silent Tears; A Journey of Hope in a Chinese
Orphanage

Chasing China; A Daughter's Quest for Truth
A Thread Unbroken

If you have enjoyed my work, I would be grateful for you to post an honest review on Amazon, Bookbub, and any other platforms you use for your books.

To those of you who have left reviews, my sincere gratitude is yours.

I would love to connect with you on Facebook, Instagram, and Twitter. Please sign up to my newsletter to be eligible to win fantastic giveaways, get news of just released books, and get a peek into the life of the Bratt Pack.

Into the Blue

A By the Sea Novel

KAY BRATT

To Heather
You Are Loved

Prologue

It was a gorgeous day on Maui, and just perfect for grabbing a chair and parking it next to the water. Many people had done just that, sitting with toes in the sand and sun on their faces, enjoying the soft breeze that was just strong enough to tickle and tease as it crept across the waves.

But the weather was deceiving. This was not a good day for Jules Monroe.

Jules pushed the sweaty strands of hair out of her eyes before dipping the sand bucket back into the ocean. The foamy water swirled and filled the bucket, and she lifted it up again, pouring it over the beached whale. Her arms were getting weak and her shoulder was throbbing, right along with the muscles that ran down her lower back. Her calves burned from straining against the current, trying to stay upright in one spot, despite the crashing waves and the ocean's pull.

But while everything hurt, she couldn't stop. Each time she thought she couldn't possibly lift another bucket of water, she gazed into that big, intelligent eye and somehow found the strength to do it again.

At times, the murmurs and clicks of photos being taken by onlookers caught her attention. She wanted to scream at them to go away. To take their voyeuristic curiosity elsewhere. To shove their selfies where the sun didn't shine. But she needed all her reserves.

Her emotions couldn't get in the way of her work.

The melon-headed whale—or blackfish, as she'd grown up calling them—were her favorites, though technically they were part of the dolphin family. She'd rarely seen them close to shore in her lifetime, as they tended to stay in deep waters.

That was how she'd known how serious the situation was when she got the call earlier. Out of the ten stranded whales, four had already been guided back out to sea, but six were still being examined and helped. The one under her ministrations had been guided out only to linger in place with no motivation to go deeper, until slowly returning to the beach. It was clear there was something terribly wrong with the cow.

Julies cringed when a spasm hit her just below her left shoulder blade. It was moments like this that reminded her she was no longer a young, vibrant beach girl.

At least she'd gotten some relief by switching from helping hold the whale up to keeping her top wet.

She focused. Filling and pouring another bucket.

Then another.

Don't think of the pain, she coaxed herself.

She reached up and caressed the bulge on the whale's forehead, the physical attribute that they were named for. The cow was only about seven feet long and probably three hundred pounds. Dark and sleek, and so very beautiful.

No one knew why the ten melon-headed whales had stranded on Sugar Beach in Kihei, but Jules suspected it was the recent increase in the Navy's sonar being used in the waters surrounding the Hawaiian Islands. The rescue team had been trying to save them for going on fifteen hours now.

"Jules." The sound of her husband Noah's soft voice momentarily broke her focus as he put his hand on her shoulder. She knew what he was going to ask her to do.

"No," she insisted, refusing to give up.

Jonah sighed loudly. His father had called him to come help, and Jules had found his calmness a welcome balm as they worked together.

But now he was taking Noah's side.

"Mom, you can't do this all day and all night. You are exhausted and we've helped enough. Let the team do their job," he urged.

"I'm not leaving her," Jules said. "She's so afraid."

Noah pulled the bucket from her hands, dropping it into the water before he took her by the shoulders and gently forced her to turn around.

"Jules, look at me. You have to let her go. Kealoha is ready to perform her death rite."

Jules swallowed hard. She felt like a failure.

Kealoha was a leader in the small community of cultural practitioners on Maui. Her mere presence on the island made the officials explore every possibility before even contemplating euthanizing any sea life. However, it was clear that from every side—cultural leaders, tourists, veterinarians, and the officials—they all wanted the same thing.

Jules had joined voices with Kealoha when she'd begged for more time to hold the whales up so they could get stronger and try to save themselves, or at least swim away and die their own dignified deaths, but the officials had set a deadline and they were now a little past it. The veterinarians had already sedated two of the whales to make them comfortable so they could humanely euthanize them.

Kealoha came into view and embraced Jules.

"Jules, they found a calf half a mile down the beach.

They're already saying its body shows signs of infection and sickness. I think the pod was guiding it in for us to help it, but they never meant to come all the way to the beach."

This cow was the mother of the calf.

There was no way to prove it, but Jules just knew it was true. She felt it. That was why she felt such a connection with this particular old girl. They were kindred spirits. Two mothers who would sacrifice their lives for their children.

And the rest of them? Easy answer—whales created a close-knit community. They would've decided it was safer to guide the calf in with a few protectors.

"I am so sorry," Kealoha whispered. "But we can at least do this for her. We will ask their ancestors and the gods to take her gently and quickly. You have shown her such courage and compassion. You've done all you can do, and now we have to let her go."

Jules knew the older woman was just as devastated about the outcome—and that they couldn't save them all. They tried, though. Every single time. It wasn't simply human kindness. For Hawaiians, the whales were deeply revered, believed to be a manifestation of Kanaloa, a famous sea god.

A few other cultural practitioners stepped into view, quiet and waiting.

Jules knew them all by name. She respected their commitment.

Behind her, the others continued to hold the whale up in the water. That group was younger—a generation removed from tradition, but still taking on their role quietly, without questions. Jules remembered the first time she'd seen such a practice on the beach. She'd only been five or six years old and her father had explained to her that whales' bodies were meant to stay afloat in water, the buoyancy keeping them weightless. When they were sick and unable to hold themselves up, they could easily crush their own organs if not assisted.

She'd given her first daughter that same lesson one early morning on a beach more than thirty years ago. Her little Nama—a sprite of a girl that she'd only had for a few years before the sea had seemingly swallowed her up too, before giving her back as an adult woman.

A gift.

So many years ago, Jules would've gone into the blue herself, following her daughter into an endless sea. But Noah had grounded her. As had Jonah.

They'd needed her too.

Jules hoped this cow didn't have more calves waiting out there, braying for their mother to return.

It took everything in her, but she finally stepped back and nodded through the tears that rained down her face.

"Okay," she whispered.

The whale was probably dehydrated, and possibly sunburned even through the wet towels they kept over her.

"We must let them end her suffering," Noah said.

Jules approached the whale again, resting her forehead on the animal's and wrapping her arms as far around the massive wet body as they could go.

She felt a shudder ripple through the whale.

"You are magnificent," she whispered. "Be at peace."

With that, she turned, her sobs erupting as Noah opened his arms and welcomed her in. She couldn't bear to watch the last minutes, so he guided her out of the water. Her son took her other arm and together, they quietly left the whale behind so that she could let go and drift into the blue.

Day One

Chapter One

Jules moved slowly and methodically, taking care not to wake Gemma. She winced at a sudden pain that shot through the back of her skull and landed right behind her left eye. But she continued the rocking motion side to side, even as she walked forward—a technique that only came with practice—and gently laid Gemma in the middle of the nest of pillows on the bed.

She kept her hands on the baby for a moment while still humming, until Gemma settled and stilled, safe in her slumber.

The throbbing in her head quit just as fast as it started, and like a panther, Jules backed out of the room and quietly pulled the door until it was nearly shut, leaving a few inches so that she could hear her youngest grandchild if she woke.

She took a deep breath and rolled her neck, then straightened her shoulders, attempting to work out a cramp. Her body still hadn't quite recovered from the abuse it took when she'd worked with the mama cow the week before. Her emotions hadn't either.

Preliminary test results on the calf showed that it had indeed been sick. Pneumonia to start, but there were other suspected issues too. Most calves die at sea, but something must've been very special about this one because the cow had risked her life to save it.

The rescue team had failed her, and the pod had lost four important members. Jules could only imagine their grieving out in the ocean as they moved on, smaller in number than before.

She sighed, pushing the memory of the cow away. She had a big day ahead of her and needed to be mentally sharp, as well as physically, if she could manage it.

Jules felt like a fairly young grandma at fifty-eight, and she was definitely healthier than most her age, but putting a child as stubborn—and heavy—as eighteen-month-old Gemma down for a nap might compete with holding a mama blackfish above the water. Jules wished she had time to go back to her daily swims in the ocean. Those brief respites from the chaos of life helped keep her physically and mentally sharp. But there just weren't enough hours in the day for that anymore.

Gemma wasn't the only grandchild filling her time, but she was the one who took the most energy. She was a little dark-headed firecracker with a streak of stubbornness. Jules wondered where she got it from because her parents sure didn't possess the same nature. Quinn was the most laid-back of her three daughters, and Gemma's father, Liam, was just as chill. However, firecracker or not, when Jules looked into the big brown eyes of her only granddaughter, she just melted, and her heart felt like it would explode with love.

Every. Single. Time.

"Is she down?" Noah asked, seeing her enter the kitchen.

"She sure is. Finally. That child sure knows how to fight sleep. I know she's nearing the terrible twos, but I think she's just the most self-willed of all our grands, and we're in it for the long haul."

Noah looked over the newspaper he held, raising his

eyebrows. "Hmm... wonder where she gets that from?"

"I was just thinking the same thing."

He tilted his head, giving her a sarcastic smile.

Jules held her hands up. "Oh no, don't blame me. I was talking about her Aunt Lani."

They both laughed.

It was funny because when Gemma's personality started emerging, everyone said her granddaughter was a lot like her. Even at just eighteen months old, Gemma showed signs of a strong willpower. But no matter how tenacious she was, Jules was immediately smitten. Gemma might be a little spoiled but having a child from Quinn to fuss over was something she'd never thought would happen.

Quinn was their little girl who had been lost at sea when she was only three years old. Jules and Noah thought she'd drowned when she'd fallen off their boat and had grieved her, but miraculously, she'd somehow made it to shore. The real tragedy was that it took nearly three decades for them to be reunited.

The circumstances of her survival and abduction didn't come forward until a few years back, when Nama returned to Maui as Quinn, an adult searching for the truth.

After being swept away at sea, Quinn was found on a beach, then was taken off the island and raised on the mainland as someone else's daughter. Only the miracle of DNA testing had helped lead her back to her real family. The irony was that Jules's own mother had been the one to keep Nama away from them, as she believed that doing so would end the family curse that she was convinced they were under.

It was a tragic story with a happy ending. But since Jules had missed most of Quinn's childhood and all of her young adulthood, she sometimes had to remind herself that Gemma wasn't Quinn, and that she needed to stop drowning her with attention and over-protectiveness.

But reminiscing on Quinn's past reminded Jules that she needed to talk to Liam, Gemma's dad, about what sort of gate he planned to install around the swimming pool they were building. She was armed with facts, including the one that drowning was ranked in the top five causes of unintentional deaths and that he and Quinn needed to be very vigilant.

Their new home—and really the entire property— was quite the showstopper because of Liam's craftsman skills, but Jules wished they'd decided against a pool. The inn they operated was only a few miles away from them, after all. They could just hop over for a swim on Quinn's days off if they wanted.

She took a deep breath, settling her nerves, and giving herself a reality check that her concerns about Gemma's well-being were entirely born of her fear that the past would somehow repeat itself. Quinn and Liam were wonderful, attentive parents. She just couldn't bear the thought of Quinn going through what she had endured after her child had been taken from her.

Jules checked the clock on the stovetop and considered the multitude of tasks she had to accomplish that day. The short respite while Gemma slept needed to be used productively.

"I'll have to wake her in forty-five minutes," she said, staring at her husband across the room. She never tired of admiring how handsomely he'd aged, his once-blond hair now glimmering with silver. His eyes had many more lines around them, but they were still a piercing blue and made her feel giddy when he looked at her just right. He'd kept a decent shape, too; his frequent swims in the ocean keeping him fit and strong.

Noah set his paper down and took a sip of his coffee. "I've got to go up to the marina and talk to the mechanic about the vibration in the hull of one of the boats, then I need to pick up our new signage to see if it's right this time. If it's a go, I have permission to hang one in Lahaina. Then I'll hit the gym. Do you want me to pick up the boys when I'm done? You could let the little empress sleep longer," Noah offered.

Jules laughed at Noah's pet name for Gemma. She had her Papa wrapped around her little finger, but she also thought he hung the sun and the moon and probably all the stars.

The laugh brought back the pain in her head and she put her hand to her eye.

"You okay?" Noah asked.

"I'm fine. This headache just keeps making short, sudden appearances." She removed her hand when the fire-quick pain faded. "Anyway, thanks, but I'll get the boys. Gemma loves to wait in the line for them to come out of school. We'll come straight home and they can help me pack sandwiches for tomorrow. They've got karate tonight, so I'll try to get them to finish their homework before Quinn gets here."

"What about asking Helen to come over today? Maybe she could help out with the kids?"

Jules shook her head, maybe a little too forcefully. "Noah, don't."

He held his hands up innocently. "She's been trying to spend more time with you, Jules. She's not going to be here forever. It might be time to cut her some slack."

Jules didn't reply. She loved her mother. Or did she? It was complicated. Her mother had pushed her away from home when she was young. As if their rocky relationship wasn't bad enough when she wasn't much more than a kid, Helen had kept Jules apart from her own daughter for so many years.

What she'd done was unforgivable.

However, Jules was a firm believer that one should let go of negative energy to salvage their own soul, so she'd forgiven her mother.

But she'd never forget.

Forgiving was one thing, but there really wasn't time to try to mend the relationship. That ship had sailed and now, Jules wanted to concentrate on her own children and grands. She'd pledged to herself many years ago that she'd be a different kind of mother than the one she'd had.

The gods must've really wanted to challenge her because motherhood wasn't an easy job. Everyone thought raising small children was hard, but for Jules, mothering her adult kids was even tougher. Guiding them without overstepping any boundaries was a constant balancing act. But as glad as she was to be there for them, she worried a lot.

Especially about her youngest daughter, Kira, who always seemed to be overwhelmed with the boys. Jules worried that they were enrolled in too many activities, but Kira was determined to raise well-rounded children. Jules wished she'd just let them be kids—give them their freedom to explore the beaches and the ocean— the beautiful natural gifts that Maui offered without a demanding schedule.

They were all much too busy. It wasn't just Kira. Jules found herself feeling more exhausted than normal lately, and her to-do list was getting longer with each passing year.

First and foremost, their family beach outreach took a lot of work. Twice a week, she and Noah packed enough sandwiches, snacks, and bottled water to hand out to the small tent towns that cropped up on several beaches.

They were the people who needed the most help, left homeless by unfortunate circumstances.

At least most of them.

No matter how they got into the predicament they were in, it was a hard life. The authorities were always chasing them off, making them remove their temporary homes to find a new place to settle. They weren't welcome anywhere, and she could only imagine how hopeless that existence felt to them. Sometimes a gesture of kindness was all they needed to renew their spirits and give them enough energy to make it another day.

She and Noah had been doing the outreach for many years, ever since their own son had been one of them when he decided to disappear from society. Jonah was doing well now, but just because they were able to bring him home didn't mean they could walk away from others like him.

"I have so much to do," she said, her voice trailing off as her eyes fell on the stack of bills she needed to pay. "I also need to do some scouting for a new crew member for Lani's boat. The new girl quit."

"Seasickness?" Noah asked.

"Nope, just doesn't want to work a real schedule. She's new to the island and hasn't shaken her Maui fever yet."

"That's the third one in a month."

Jules nodded, then sighed. "I know. I need to find someone who's a native or at least more established here. Someone dependable."

"I agree. Maybe we need to advertise online." Noah stood and came to her, opening his arms wide for Jules to fall into. She did and took a moment to breathe in his scent and just be still. They were supposed to be semi-retired, but they were busier now than back when they manned their charters full-time.

They parted and Jules felt a rush of exhaustion and

wished for the warmth of his arms again. More than thirty years together and they were still solid. More than solid—they were crazy about each other. For a moment, she wished they could just go behind closed doors and spend the rest of the morning in each other's arms.

Instead, she smiled at him.

"I love you, Noah."

"Right back at you, my Jules of the Sea," he said. He looked worried. "Are you okay today?"

She nodded. "I'm fine. Just trying to keep this headache at bay. And I'm tired. Might be coming down with something."

"You need to fit in some rest, Jules. You know we can't do without you. And those kids need to give you a break."

"I'm fine. I love helping with my grandbabies. It's the best part of my day." And it was true. Yes, sometimes she was tired and wished for more time to relax, but she wouldn't have it any other way. Her children and her grands needed her—and that was a blessing.

But her blessings took up a lot of time, and Jules remembered that the weekly payroll for their two boats was due in less than two days. It used to be her favorite task—her gift for numbers making her a vital part of the family business. But now, Jules was finding it harder to juggle her many responsibilities, and the time constraints made balancing out her rows of numbers a little less fun.

Noah smiled. "Alright, but don't even think about cooking tonight. I'm taking you out for a romantic dinner. Just you and me at a table with an ocean view. Dessert will be a long, luxurious massage by yours truly. With candlelight."

He winked and she laughed. Dinner out would be wonderful. A massage would be even better. After all these years together, he knew her body better than she did.

Noah leaned in for a kiss, then grabbed his keys from the bowl on the counter and slipped out the back door.

Jules went to her laptop and hit the start button, then went to switch the clothes from the washer to the dryer while the computer loaded up. She needed to put on her multi-tasking hat and move fast, as she was down to just over half an hour before Gemma would be up and demanding that the world do her bidding.

And of course, Jules would do her best. Because as she'd learned over the last few years and three grand-children, that's what grandparents were put on earth to do.

Chapter Two

Fifteen minutes later, Jules's phone rang. She lunged to grab it before it woke Gemma. If the little empress didn't get her full nap in, she'd be hard to handle for the rest of the afternoon.

Her son's face popped up and she answered. He didn't usually call this time of day.

"Hi, Jonah. What's up?"

"Mom, have you talked to Kira?"

"No. Why?" Jules sensed worry in Jonah's voice, and she sat down with the phone, her eyes on the hallway in case Gemma appeared.

"I saw her this morning for a late breakfast, but she didn't show up for the three o'clock charter," he said, sounding worried. "She never said anything to me about skipping out. Her phone is going straight to voicemail, so the boat had to leave without her. Michael called me having a meltdown because it's a group of college kids hellbent on getting wasted and he can't reach her."

"Oh, no. He really needed Kira today."

"Damn straight," Jonah said. "She knows better than that."

"That's really strange, though. She always has her phone on in case I need her about the kids. Did she say anything at your breakfast? Was she upset?" Jules asked.

"Not that I could tell. She was a little more quiet than usual, but she said she was just tired because she'd been up late helping Micah with a school project. Some kind of complicated volcano thing."

"Okay, I'll try to call her," Jules said. "I'll bet she and Michael had an argument over whose turn it was to oversee the school project, so she's just gone silent."

"You're probably right," he said. "Listen, I'm supposed to be hooking up some new water heaters for Quinn, but first I'm going to take a look around some of Kira's running spots to see if I can find her car."

"Okay, but don't get Quinn shook up. She's got a lot on her plate this week since that celebrity from *Hawaii Five-O* is staying at the inn this weekend."

"She won't even know I'm gone."

"Call me if you find Kira," Jules said, feeling the headache coming back. She put her hand over her eye, as though to slow the pain.

"I will."

They hung up and Jules immediately dialed Kira. Just as Jonah said, it went to voicemail on the first ring. Jules waited for the beep.

"Kira, this is mom. Call me as soon as you get this." She was worried. It wasn't like her daughter to just go off the radar and especially not to show up for work.

Jules was thankful that, for the most part, her family respected the roles each had in the business and got along well. Of course, there was always going to be small stuff and petty disagreements, but she'd worked hard to give her children a solid foundation built on love and trust; the opposite of what she'd experienced in her own home growing up.

If only there was a way to fully heal her son's soul. Jonah was better now, but he lacked a sense of purpose. Jules knew that he needed to figure out what he was most passionate about, and then do more of it. As a mother, she wished she could tell him what it was. But that was his journey, not hers.

She rose and went to the bedroom door, making sure Gemma was still asleep, then went back to the family room and sat down. She hoped that everything would be ironed out before it was time to pick up the boys. They sure didn't need to worry about their mom.

Jules always worried about her girls, but Kira usually didn't take center stage in the drama department. Not that she hadn't given them any trouble growing up, but now that she was a married mom of two, she was responsible and barely made any ripples.

Except for a few years ago, when she and Michael expressed a wish to leave the family business and go out on their own. Jules would've supported it if they'd been in a position to afford it. She and Noah had started with nothing and it hadn't been easy. When they were Kira's age, they'd carried debt that caused many a sleepless night, and they didn't want their daughter to carry the same burden. Not when Jules and Noah were more than happy to share the success of the family business with all of their children and their families.

They'd worked it out and as far as Jules knew, Kira and Michael were happy with the changes and were saving for the day that they could branch out on their own if they still wished to.

However, with a daughter like Kira, it was hard to know how she was really feeling. She kept everything inside, filing away her worries so no one would think she couldn't handle her own life. It made being her mother a little complicated, because Jules always craved to deepen their communication, a gift of love that she and her mother never had.

Her daughter Lani was the opposite. She was more

than happy to blast the world with her grievances, and always be a loud advocate for the underdog and any revolutionary endeavors. She was the tough one, physically and emotionally, and Jules didn't know where she'd inherited that from, even though she admired her for it.

The relationship she had with each of her kids was different, yet strong, and she was proud of them. Her children would never have to wonder if their mother loved them. It was evident in everything she did and everything she was.

The phone rang, disrupting her reverie, and Jules jumped for it.

"Hello?"

"Mom? What is going on?" asked Lani.

Jules sighed. She'd hoped Lani had news of her sister. "Jonah called you?"

"No, Michael did. And he never calls me, so I know he's really worried. I barely got anything out of him before he lost signal and the call dropped. Where do you think she is?"

"I don't know, Lani. This isn't like her and I'm worried."

She could hear the fear in Lani's voice. "Me too, Mom."

Her phone beeped and Jules held the device out to see who it was.

"That's Jonah calling back. Let me get it."

She switched over.

"Jonah?"

"Mom," he said, "I think we have a problem. I found Kira's car but she's nowhere around."

Jules sat back on the couch. She could feel her pulse begin to race, and the fear that stuck in her throat made it hard to speak.

"Where is it?" She finally got out.

"In front of the Makawao Reserve. She does run there sometimes but the weird thing is that her wallet and phone are in plain sight on the front seat."

Jules glanced at the clock. Fifteen minutes until it was time to wake Gemma. "And she always carries her phone, even when she's jogging. Doesn't she? Something's wrong, Jonah. I feel it."

"I'm calling the police to meet me out here. I'll call you back as soon as I can. I'll call Dad too." Jonah said.

Jules had one more thing to tell him, but he was gone. And suddenly, she couldn't even think of what that was. As she stared at the phone in her hand, she began to feel detached, as though her arm wasn't part of her body and she had no control. She was going to call someone, and it was important, but who? Or was she supposed to meet someone? There was something… but she couldn't put her finger on it.

The blinding pain was back, but this time it pounded just behind her eyes like a sledgehammer. She dropped the phone, or rather, her fingers dropped the phone without her telling them to, as though they'd lost all gripping abilities.

As she breathed deeper and deeper, reality as she knew it began to fade into blurred lines and energy, she and the space around her becoming one. Slowly, and somewhat euphorically, she slipped into the blue.

Chapter Three

Jonah paced the parking lot near Kira's car, waiting for Noah. He tried to knock the mud off his boots by stomping against the pavement. He'd already gone at least a mile up the trail and back looking for Kira, but he'd found no signs of her. The reserve was more than two thousand acres and even trying to gauge where she could be felt like looking for a needle in a haystack.

A man and woman hiking with a dog passed by him, but that was it.

He wished his dad would hurry up. Being in the jungle had set off something in his head. Something he didn't like. It had opened a door best left closed. And locked.

Sometimes, in the quiet, his mind crawled back to memories he tried to keep buried. Testing the waters, his conscience slipped that secret door open and peeked in, seeing if the pain and guilt were still there, clinging to him like a bad rash.

Iraq was a million miles away in reality, but right around the detour in his mind, sitting smack dab in the middle of a dead end. He could never unsee the things he'd seen, including the memories of an especially gruesome day. A day when he'd been the sole survivor. The outcome was a miracle or a curse, depending on how he was feeling in the moment.

He hated thinking about Iraq and everything that had happened there. If there was a surgery that would carve out every last memory from duty, he'd be the first in line. He never talked to anyone about his experience. He didn't seek help, though he probably should have. He preferred to avoid exploring his emotions, and while he may have seemed okay on the outside, it was a mirage.

He would probably never be okay again.

He remembered the day he told his family he'd enlisted and the sudden silence around their usually chaotic supper table—the look of fear in his mother's eyes that pierced him deeply and made him look away.

"But you're only eighteen," she whispered.

"It's what I want to do," he replied. *What I need to do*, he'd said to himself.

"You'll come back a man that's for sure," his father had finally said, his voice hoarse with tears. He'd picked up a napkin and wiped his face as he stood up then walked outside, leaving the rest of his dinner untouched on the plate.

His mother had tried to smooth it over.

"Jonah, are you sure? We can talk to someone. Tell them you made a mistake."

"It's done, Mom."

She sighed long and deep.

"Girls, please go to your rooms for a few minutes," she'd said.

When they were out of earshot she sat back in her chair, her chin in her hands as she looked into his eyes. Jonah knew she was trying to think of a way to change his mind. He remained stiff. Unyielding.

But he could feel his ears burning, the heat putting a sheen of sweat over his lip.

"Your father—he, well—you know how he feels about war," she said.

He did know. His dad was a gentle man who had the utmost respect for every living thing. From the time he was a boy, his dad had taught him that every human and living creature had a right to exist and that Jonah was always to tread carefully so as to not prematurely end a life.

So many spiders they'd shepherded out of the house for a chance at freedom amidst the screams of his sisters.

Moths and geckos too.

Even when they caught a fish, his father taught Jonah to first thank the fish for his life, then the ocean for bringing the fish to them for sustenance. He killed the fish efficiently and immediately, never allowing it to suffer. And they never fished for sport. Years later, when the family could've made big money taking people out deep-sea fishing, Jonah knew it wasn't even a question in his father's mind. He would take them to snorkel. To dive. And to view the magnificence of the magical life under the sea.

But never to kill just for sport.

His father's approval—or more likely, his disapproval—was part of the reason Jonah had thought so hard about signing up. He'd been quietly torn over the decision for two years prior. He never wanted to hurt his parents. He wanted to make them proud. But he'd been fighting an invisible enemy since he was a little boy, after his sister was ripped from his grasp and disappeared under the pounding waves.

Everyone said it wasn't his fault, but their words rang hollow back then and still did every time he'd heard them since.

Kira—his shadow, as his parents liked to call her—had cried herself to sleep once she realized what his service meant—that she might not see her big brother for some time, or maybe ever again.

Those big eyes pooling with tears had slayed him. He'd wanted to yell at her and tell her to stop idolizing him, that he wasn't worth it. He'd already failed one sister—a sister that because of him, she'd never known—and he'd let down his parents.

But he had to give it to the pesky little shit. She'd sworn she'd write every day and damn if she hadn't. The childhood devotion from his baby sister had been what had kept him going on the lonely and despairing nights when he wished a stray round would come his way—and on the days when what his eyes saw was more than his soul could take.

Then before he knew it, it was all over.

The long flights home had earned him an epiphany. He realized that there was no outrunning his demons. They'd followed him and tailed his every step through the hot valley of hell and were still sitting in the seat beside him the whole way home.

At least he'd made it out alive. But he wasn't back six months before he'd turned to drugs to numb the pain he couldn't outrun. Thankfully, he'd found a way to get clean on his own. But not without significant damage to the relationship he had with his parents. He saw how they watched him now, the fear and sadness he'd brought to their eyes.

But not Kira. She never looked at him like she expected him to relapse, and she didn't scrutinize him for signs. She saw him as the older brother who would always be her hero.

And he didn't want to fail her now.

"KIRA!? KIRA...!" He whistled the secret shrill they'd used as children when they'd played in the woods.

The birds mocked him.

His dad pulled up, sliding into the parking lot too quickly and screeching to a stop. He was already pelting out questions before his feet hit the pavement and the door slammed behind him.

"What's going on?"

"She didn't show up for work and doesn't answer her phone," Jonah said. "I met her at Colleen's for a late breakfast this morning and she seemed fine. I guess."

"You guess?" Noah asked as he circled Kira's car, peering into the windows without touching anything. He cursed when he spotted the wallet and phone on the seat.

"I think we should break the window," Jonah said. "If she doesn't have a passcode on her phone, we can see her last text messages. That should tell us something."

"That's not a good idea."

"Why?"

"Because if there really is something wrong, the police will want the inside of the car untouched so they can sweep it for clues. If we break in and most likely can't even get on her phone, it will be for nothing and we'll have our fingerprints all over everything. Let's focus on what you know. How did she seem this morning?"

Jonah pulled his hands through his hair. "Fine. I mean, she said she was tired. She looked exhausted. But other than that, she just wanted to talk about me."

"What about you?" Noah asked, turning to look at him. "Do we have two dramas going on today?"

"No. Not at all. Same, same. You know, she wanted to know if I'm ever going to settle down—if Kim is the one. Told me to stop dragging my feet. All that stuff she won't let up about."

Jonah hated it when his sisters pressured him about his current girlfriend, Kim. If it was meant to be, it would be. To be honest, he thought Kim was out of his league and it was only a matter of time before she realized it and left him for some golden boy with a medical degree. She was on a trajectory that would one day put her on a much higher level, with her doctorate in her pocket and stars in her eyes. Jonah didn't want to get too invested when he knew that fate was coming. He was just a simple island man. And he had issues that he couldn't expect anyone to commit to. Especially someone as special as Kim.

His sisters needed to stop bugging him about it.

Noah rolled his eyes. "What exactly did Michael say? I can't get him on the phone."

"He's too far out for a signal now. He told me she'd mentioned last night about going for a jog before work. I asked him if she was mad about something and he swears she wasn't. But I'm not completely convinced."

"Now don't go jumping to conclusions," Noah said. "Even if they were arguing, it's not like your sister to just ignore her responsibilities. Did you tell him you found her car?"

Jonah nodded.

Noah looked disappointed, then took out his phone. He made short order of leaving a message for Michael, telling him to call immediately when his charter was over.

He hung up and slipped the phone back into his pocket.

"What about the boys?" Jonah asked.

"Mom is picking them up from school."

Just then, a police car pulled up and parked beside them.

"Well, this just turned serious, but I hope we don't really need them," Jonah said as the officer climbed out.

"Better safe than sorry," his dad said, then went to shake hands. "I'm Noah Monroe. This is my son, Jonah. We called because we're concerned about my daughter,

Kira. She didn't show up for work. This is her car."

"Don't touch anything just in case we're dealing with a crime scene," the cop said, waving them back a few feet.

Jonah felt sick to his stomach.

He looked at his dad and could tell that Noah also cringed at the words. Calling this a potential crime scene was not what they wanted or expected, though Noah had alluded to just that when discussing breaking the window.

The look on his dad's face sent Jonah back in time. Way, way back to a fated day on the ocean when he was told that Nama had been lost at sea. He hoped more than anything that Kira hadn't disappeared on them.

Jonah should've been looking out for her better too.

"I'm Officer Kaopuiki. Want to tell me what's going on?" The officer asked, taking a pad and pen out of his pocket. "Give me your names again."

"Noah Monroe, and my son, Jonah."

The officer looked up. "Monroe? The same ones with the daughter who has the inn up in Hana? Owners of one of the charter businesses out of Lahaina?"

Jonah knew where he was going, and he didn't like it. They'd barely avoided a media circus when Quinn had returned to Maui and discovered that she was his long-lost sister. Especially because his mom was a Rocha and many years ago his great-grandfather had dishonored a Maui family. His grandmother and his parents had more than made up for it with other humanitarian efforts on the island, but it seemed they'd never outrun the stories that had become even more exaggerated over the years.

"Yes, Quinn is my daughter too," Noah said, his expression impassive. "I've got three here on the island."

The officer hesitated, then stood back and looked at them, as though contemplating their story. "Let me take a look at the car," he said, tucking the pad and pen back into his pocket.

He walked around the car, peering into the driver's window without touching it.

Then he squatted at the front of the car, looking under it.

"It's been here awhile," he said. "The condensation puddle has evaporated."

Jonah bit back a sarcastic remark.

The officer stood and made his way to the back of the car. He pulled at the trunk, then knocked on it as though someone might knock back.

That dried up Jonah's feeling of sarcasm really quick.

When the officer squatted there and looked under the back, he gave a satisfied grunt and stood up, waving a set of keys.

"She left her keys," he said. "That means she must've left her car willingly."

"Or someone else parked it here and left it to be found," Noah said.

"Open the trunk," Jonah said, that sick feeling growing larger inside his chest.

"Was just going to do that," the officer said.

He found the key and lifted the trunk, and they all peered in.

Thank God, she wasn't in there. All Jonah saw was the usual family stuff. A blanket. A roll of paper towels, and a half-empty jug of motor oil.

"You going to open the doors and get out her phone?" Jonah asked.

"We'll get to that. I'm following protocol here. Don't rush the process. There're also rules against invading privacy without cause. First we need to make sure there's cause."

This time Jonah fought the urge to give him a good

thump under his weak chin.

The officer closed the trunk and took out the pen and pad again.

"Can you give me your missing daughter's name, date of birth, and a description?"

Noah filled him in while Jonah texted a few of his and Kira's mutual friends to see if any of them had gone with her for a hike or jog.

Seen Kira today? The ones who replied all had the same answer.

No, why?

Behind him, his dad filled in the officer on Kira's tattoos and the scar she has just under her left eye from the time they were kids and he'd popped her with a rock with his brand-new slingshot. It wasn't on purpose and he'd never let her know how guilty he felt every time she was tired, and the scar became more visible.

He felt nausea rising within him.

Revisiting childhood memories would lead to nowhere good. Jonah had also been the last person to see his sister Quinn before she'd disappeared so many years ago. There were some who'd blamed him. Suspicion followed him for years.

And guilt had plagued him too.

Now here he was again, the last person to have seen Kira. What was it with him and losing the people around him? It was like he was cursed.

"Jonah!"

He turned.

"You didn't hear me? I've called your name at least three times," his dad said.

"Sorry. What?" He approached.

"The officer has some questions for you."

"Your dad said you were the last to see your sister. I need all the details. Start from the beginning of your day," the officer said, flipping his pad to a new page.

Jonah sighed long and hard, reminding himself to remain cordial and not let the officer ruffle him into looking guilty, then he began to recap the day.

When he was done, the officer looked sufficiently bored. "Make sure no one gets around the car in case we need to take prints."

"Can't you do it now?" Noah asked.

"It's not official yet. Lots of Maui locals head into this reserve to get away from the rush of tourists for a while," he said. "My bet is she'll be out before dark. You folks don't need to get all riled up because she's gone quiet for a few hours. She's an adult, after all."

Jonah hoped with all he had that the officer was right. But in his gut—deep down where he usually buried everything—he knew that something was wrong.

Chapter Four

Helen stood in the garden and looked at the weeds growing around her hibiscus bush. It was an old one, now reaching over seven feet tall as it bloomed over the stone wall. Her gardener, George, liked it because the leaves shed so slowly that it wasn't hard to maintain the area around it. He tended to leave that corner alone for the most part, which was why he'd obviously missed some maintenance.

George would be there in the morning and she made a mental note to show him. He had been with her for more than ten years and though he'd retired from most of his other clients, he continued to come and keep everything nice for her. She supposed he believed in the idea of helping widows or some such. He even went out and bought groceries for her when the weather was bad and kept an eye on her car, letting her know when she needed new tires or a tune-up.

When she'd first hired him, he'd praised her for what she alone had done with her garden, and Helen couldn't help but be quietly proud. Just outside her lanai was quite a show of lush plants and flowers that had been the envy of all their friends long ago. After her husband died, she'd spent most of her waking hours there, burying her complicated feelings in the very earth she tended. While she'd experienced moments of deep sorrow and loneliness in the wake of his death, there was also an intoxicating freedom that she'd never known.

It was her first time living alone. As a young woman, she'd gone straight from her parents' household and strict supervision to her husband's. And he'd been no less controlling than her father. Maybe even a little worse, if that was possible.

Helen had carefully hidden her relief at his wake.

The only place she'd let her true emotions show was in the privacy of her garden, ironically on the bench in front of the enchanting stone wall–the only piece of her sanctuary that her late husband had ever had a part in. He'd surprised her with the truckload of old stones pulled from an abandoned property a client of his owned, then paid a crew to put them into place.

Despite his grating self-congratulations, she had to admit that once completed, she loved the look of the wall. Helen had known exactly what sorts of plants and flowers would add to the beauty around it. The old stones gave the garden a look that could have never been accomplished without them and working there nearly always left her feeling spiritual.

Those were happy times over the years, on her knees, with her hands in the soil. As she'd worked, she marveled that she was finally on her own. Without having someone to wait on and demand her full time and attention, she'd put everything she had into anything she could make grow. And grow it did. Into such a show-stopper.

Her very own little peaceful paradise.

But now she only walked through and looked at her garden instead of working it. Her knees—among an assortment of other body parts—ached too much to be bending or squatting.

Growing old wasn't for sissies that was for sure. Her mind was still sharp as ever and never failed to keep a multitude of lists going, tasks that her body didn't have enough energy to complete.

There was always a tug-of-war going on up there. Perhaps the cruelty of the two opposite fates of body and mind were her penance for all the sins she'd committed in her life.

Enough of that kind of thought. It wouldn't help her state of mind at all. The years went by and she could've remarried and had another long relationship, but she vowed to never let another person have dominion over her again.

She pulled a blossom from her Awapuhi Ginger bush and squeezed it in her hand, then held it to her face and inhaled deeply.

Heavenly.

This was the one plant that her yard man despised, as it grew so fast and furious. It was only a foot or so tall when she'd first planted it. Her boys had dug the hole before they were even teenagers. Now a bit bossy and unruly, she still kept it, simply because her granddaughter Kira visited once in a blue moon to pick up some of the blooms to make her own shampoo.

It had been a while, though.

Kira was the most free-spirited of all her grandchildren. She was definitely a child of Maui with her commitment to saving ocean life and teaching others to respect their island. She was an old soul and held on to many of the nearly forgotten Hawaiian legends and lore. Helen was quite proud of her, truth be told. But she'd never let the others know that she felt Kira was a tad bit more special. Not more loved—just more special.

Helen went toward the back of the garden and sat down on the stone bench. Quietly, she said an old

Hawaiian proverb of protection as she stared at the flat stone that marked the grave of a child she'd lost—her firstborn who had been gone so long that no one other than her even remembered. Or at least no one ever spoke of it. She swallowed past the lump that came up, that no amount of time could tamp down. She reminded herself that the gods had only taken one of her children and left her three. For that, she needed to be thankful.

"Come on, Cinder, it's time for you to eat." She led the rounded pug into the house and fixed her a bowl of boiled fish and rice, then put it down and watched it disappear faster than you would think possible.

"Finished so quick?"

The tiny black pug looked up at her and Helen felt a small smile tug at the side of her mouth. She extinguished it quickly, but oh how she loved the chubby dog that over the last nearly two years had become her constant companion.

The dog was found in a dumpster by Quinn's friend, Maggie.

Helen put some food in her own bowl, grabbed a spoon, and went to the table, setting it down next to her book of crossword puzzles.

The one she'd started yesterday was almost finished. They hadn't been printing any complex ones lately.

Boring. There were only so many crossword puzzles one could do.

It was ironic. The house used to echo with noise, and she'd complained. She wished she'd known then what she knew now—that though she had been exhausted most of the time, those were the good 'ole days. The world had gotten a lot less chaotic but a lot more isolated since her children were no longer under her roof.

She'd spoiled them. Everyone knew that.

To this day, they still wanted only the finest things—

the most luxurious vacations and the biggest houses. Except for Jules.

Oddly, Jules had grown up resenting the fact that she had more than her friends or neighbors, as though being privileged embarrassed her. When it came time for her to apply for her driver's license, she'd turned down any car-buying adventures, choosing instead to hitch a ride with friends down to her favorite beaches and taking her bike anywhere else.

A snippet of color on the floor under the fridge caught her eye.

She rose from her chair, listening to her bones crack and pop before she went over and pulled it out.

It was a photo of Jules that had been lost for years.

In it, a young and beaming Jules was holding hands with her little boy, Jonah, and Nama was on her shoulders, with blue rolling waves behind them.

The picture had been taken shortly before Nama had been lost at sea. Before Helen had made the worst decision of her life and put a wall between her and Jules, probably forever.

Why hadn't she noticed the photo under there before? It had been missing for years and Helen actually thought Jules had taken it. Was it some sort of sign?

She remembered a time long ago when she'd been standing in the kitchen preparing dinner for herself and her husband. She'd had a pain that felt like a knife in her gut. With it came a vision of Jules, who had left home months before to live on the beach with Noah. She was still young but old enough that the law couldn't intervene. Helen had a lot of contacts back then and knew that Jules and Noah were trying to start their own business but were struggling.

The sudden worry over Jules, combined with the pain in her stomach, had her reaching out immediately. A mother's instinct wasn't anything to play around with. She'd arranged for some friends of hers to book an afternoon fishing trip with Noah. Of course, they were sworn to secrecy and they'd reported back that the couple was doing fine, and that Noah was a lovely young man.

They'd talked of how in love Jules had seemed.

It wasn't what Helen had wanted to hear at the time. As a mother, she'd hoped the relationship was a short-lived fling. But at least she'd known that the money she'd paid for the excursion, along with the healthy tip, had probably helped her daughter get by for a short time.

Jules had never been the wiser and Helen had done similar acts over the years until their business was thriving and healthy, and she no longer had to worry about where her daughter's next meal was coming from.

So many years ago. How she wished now she'd have done things differently. But the past was just that and it didn't do her any good to digress.

Now she pulled her laptop closer and hit the spacebar. The screen lit up, still on Facebook as she'd left it earlier. She refreshed, then scanned through Jules's page.

Nothing new.

She scanned the news feed, looking at recent photos Kira had posted of the boys. Micah and Lukas loved to pose. Little hams, they were. Micah looked a lot like his grandfather, though Helen never pointed that out. Further down, Kira had linked to an event to clean the beaches. Helen wished she could go, if only to be around people and conversation.

Helen was careful not to comment or react to anything her family posted. She didn't want any of them to know she was looking.

She doubted they thought of her very often, other than when she was standing right in front of them at the Sunday lunches Jules had made into a tradition. Even then she felt invisible. No one was interested in anything she had to say, so she didn't talk much.

Cinder grunted like a little piglet—her signal that she wanted attention.

It was amusing.

"You have a new gray hair, Cinder."

That was their inside joke. Both of them had more gray hair than could be counted. That was something that cemented their relationship. They were also both a little hefty in the cargo department. Or at least Cinder was now, after living like a little queen with all her home-cooked meals and baked treats.

At first, Helen hadn't even wanted the pathetic pup. She'd only agreed to foster the little hippo-shaped creature until a proper home could be found. Quinn had asked her to take on the favor, and how could Helen tell her granddaughter no after all she'd put her through?

She'd thought a few weeks of fostering would be easy enough, gain her some brownie points, and then the dog would leave and she would go back to her quiet, solitary life.

As the days passed, Helen found that she and her furry companion had a lot in common. Cinder had been thrown away because she was old. She probably didn't have all that many years left and those that she did have would be spent hobbling around as she tried to ignore the fact that her body had let her down.

Cinder had started off sleeping in the laundry room with the door closed.

Helen didn't want to deal with any nastiness like puddles on her fine rugs, or dog hair strewn across her bamboo floors.

They had never had dogs inside the home when she was growing up. Her father wouldn't allow it, claiming that animals were meant for outdoors. That was what he'd taught them.

So, she figured she'd foster the dog and it would be fed and taken care of, while doing her business right outside the laundry room door at the back lanai.

It had remained that way for nearly a week. Cinder's needs were taken care of without any of that pampering she'd seen some of the women around the island do with their animals. Eat. Out the door. Empty bladder. In the door. Go to sleep.

No nonsense.

However, despite the isolation, each time that Helen checked on the little dog, she appeared to be ecstatic to see her.

It had been a long time since someone—or something—was happy to see her. One evening, a terrible storm was making its way through the area. Helen had always been afraid of thunder and lightning. She wondered if Cinder was also frightened and thought she'd check on her for just a second. Helen peeked in the laundry room, ever so quietly, and the little dog peered up at her. If that wasn't a smile on its upturned snout, she'd be darned.

Cinder rose slowly and came to the door. Her tiny, bobbed tail wiggled back and forth, as though to invite Helen into her space.

Helen decided to accept. It was quiet in there, and the company of one small dog was better than enduring the storm in a whole house with no one else in it.

She worked her way down to the floor and sat against her dryer, which she'd turned on just for more noise, but the warmth of the machine mixed with that of Cinder's tongue gently kissing her wrist had touched something deep within her.

It had been decades since she'd felt comforted by anyone. Or anything.

When the storm passed, she picked up Cinder and went to the bedroom. She plopped the dog on the end of her bed, right on top of the expensive covering she'd ordered from a well-known designer in Oahu.

"Do you want to stay in here with me or not? The storm might circle around and come back, you know."

Cinder looked up at her as though in disbelief, then circled a few times and settled into a sleeping position, before giving a little sigh and closing her eyes.

"Fine," Helen told her. "You stay down here, and I'll stay on my side. And we'll get along just fine. Tomorrow we go back to normal."

She'd gone to bed expecting to wake up the next morning and return to their old routine.

Cinder in the laundry room with scheduled feedings and outside breaks timed out to the minute.

However, sometime in the wee hours just past midnight, the storm had started back up again, and the little dog had curled up right next to Helen's legs. The warmth she'd brought traveled up Helen's body, right to the heart that she'd thought had grown cold over the years.

She thought back to her father, who was long gone—six feet in the ground—his gravesite never once visited by Helen. Despite his feelings toward animals, this was her house, and her father would never tell her what to do again. Now Cinder was like a child to her.

"Want to watch a movie, Cinder?"

So here she was, having full conversations with her dog.

If the ladies from her book club could see her now, they'd laugh Helen right out of the room. She actually hadn't seen them in ages. But maybe they were like her, and their own lives weren't so fulfilled after all. Maybe that was just what they all wanted each other to believe.

"Who cares what they think, old girl? Let's go get cozy. Just you and me."

Chapter Five

Jules awoke to a cold sensation on her lips and opened her eyes to discover that she was laid out on the kitchen floor.

A small child, who Jules didn't recognize, squatted over her.

"Up," the girl said, her expression going from determined to worry. She sat down on the floor and stared at Jules.

Jules didn't like the worried look on the child's face, so she slowly turned over on her side and struggled to pull her legs up to her middle. She needed to get up. But how?

She wanted to comfort the girl. What was her name?

Jules thought and thought but could not remember. A flash of memory came and went, a small bundle being put in her arms, tears making warm tracks down her face. Gratitude. A crushing love.

Whether she knew her or not, Jules felt strongly that the child's well-being was in her hands. Something wasn't right. She needed to get help.

She needed her phone.

Slowly, she looked above and around her and willed herself to get up.

When her limbs finally obeyed, she sat upright and

moved onto her hands and knees. It took a few more authoritative commands for her body to fully stand.

She wavered back and forth, then put out a hand on the counter to stabilize herself. She felt numb in so many places. Her arm. Her foot.

Jules went to the phone and picked it up.

Just then, a small noise rang out and a box opened on the screen where Jules knew there should be words. All she saw was a series of lines and squiggles.

She tried to concentrate. The box faded, then the throbbing returned. This time worse than before. She needed help. The screen of the phone lit up again as she touched it, but where to go from there wasn't clear.

The child let out a louder cry. One that intensified the throbbing in Jules's head. Then a series of noises came from the phone.

More darts that felt as though they were penetrating her brain.

She dropped the phone, her hands going to her ears.

The clatter of the phone hitting the table and bouncing off the tiled floor was enough to quiet the child, but Jules saw the screen was now shattered.

Strangely, she didn't feel any frustration.

If anything, she was puzzled, wondering what to do next. She was aware that everything she should do required a sequence of actions, but she just couldn't pinpoint what they were or how to do them.

She did, however, feel a sense of calm that everything would work out. Well, everything that she could remember, which wasn't a lot.

This new feeling of peace was intoxicating. She could think about one thing. Just one. Not a myriad of things. Tasks. Chores. Memories.

All gone.

Just one thought at a time.

Kira.

Missing.

Nama.

Missing.

Fear snaked down her spine like a cold river of water.

She stared at the phone on the floor, willing it to tell her what to do. Her brain felt exhausted as she tried to force it to think.

The child had quieted and gone to the living room where she'd climbed onto the couch and pulled a blanket up to her chin.

Jules felt weary.

She lay her head on the table and allowed herself to slip away again, back into the warm silence of nothing.

Chapter Six

Jonah slid his phone into his back pocket and faced his dad. He didn't know what was in the air today, but now his mom wasn't answering her phone either. That was weird. She always answered.

"Mom's not picking up."

Noah looked at his watch. "She should be back from picking up the boys by now. They're probably harassing her over a peanut butter sandwich."

Jonah could just see it, too. The boys kept Jules hopping, right along with the little firecracker Gemma, who insisted on getting the bulk of the attention.

He looked at his phone. Kim had called multiple times. Quickly, he fired off a text telling her he'd touch base in a little while. She'd be irritated but would understand once he explained what was going on. He put his phone back in his pocket.

He was feeling overwhelmed after being grilled by the police officer. The officer had wanted every detail, even down to what Kira had ordered at Colleen's. He'd asked for witnesses, too, as though Jonah was somehow behind his sister's sudden disappearance.

Other than the harried waitress, Jonah didn't know who the hell saw them at Colleen's. It was always a madhouse there at that hour. Jonah wasn't the most social person, either. He was there to eat. He didn't usually even go out for meals—crowds weren't his thing—but Kira had called and said she'd like to see him, not for anything important—just because she missed him.

The officer wanted to see that text message too.

"Isn't that unusual?" the officer asked.

"Not really. I mean, she's got a busy life, so we don't get together one-on-one very often," Jonah answered. "But we see each other every Sunday for family dinners."

"Why did she want to fit you into her busy schedule *today*?" The officer pressed.

"Uh… I don't know. Maybe because all my sisters think it's their personal mission to keep me in line," Jonah tried but failed to keep the sarcasm out of his tone.

That statement had led into more conversation about the type of person Kira was and whether there was a possibility that she'd try to disappear on purpose. Which there wasn't. The officer also asked for the receipt from Colleen's and smirked when Jonah told him he'd paid cash and didn't get one.

Jonah had gotten angry then, and Noah made him walk away to cool off.

His dad, always the anchor and the calm in the storm. Jonah could never reconcile the man with the supposedly wild beach boy that his grandmother said stole Jules away when she was barely more than a girl.

The officer was finally satisfied and moved off to call in some details. He said he was going to file the report but that it was much too early in the game to call in the troops for a search.

Jonah dug his hands in his pockets to keep from strangling the pompous officer as he sauntered slowly to his car, not a care in the world.

"So, what do we do now?" he asked Noah, his frustration beginning to show.

"Well, we can't just stand around and wait for something to happen. If her car is here, then she's here. That's what I think."

"Or maybe she met someone here and they carpooled somewhere else," Jonah said. He knew he was grasping at straws.

"What do you mean she met someone here?" his dad asked. "Who would she meet or where would she go that's so important that she wouldn't show up for work? Or that she'd put all of us through this much worry? You know better than that, Jonah."

They leaned against Jonah's beat-up truck, both of them thinking hard as they stared at the trailhead leading into the reserve.

"I probably need to go help your mom out with the kids. I imagine that once Michael gets your messages, he'll come straight here from the dock instead of going to pick up the boys. If Quinn's there, I'll ask her to stay with your mom and the kids and I'll come back."

Jonah nodded. As soon as he was alone again, he was going back in there to look for any clues as to Kira's whereabouts. Maybe there were still some hikers who'd seen her.

"Don't go in there looking for her, Jonah," his dad said. "She might come out and you'll miss her."

Damn, he always did that. Since Jonah was a kid, his dad could read his mind like he was some kind of wizard.

"Dad, I'm going in. I'll take it slow and methodically this time. What if she's hurt in there? I'm not waiting for the MPD to say sufficient time has gone by before they'll help look. It could be too late by then."

Noah shook his head then reached over and patted Jonah's shoulder. "Be careful, son. Keep your phone on you and check it when you come out. You probably won't get a signal the deeper you go."

A phone rang and they both reached for theirs.

"It's mine," Noah said, hitting the accept button and saying hello.

Jonah watched as his father's expression slowly went from resigned to panicked.

"Okay, I'm coming right now," he said, then hung up. He looked at Jonah. "That was the office at the school. The administrator has the boys with her because your mom didn't show up and she couldn't reach her or Michael or Kira. She had my number as the fourth in line to call in an emergency. I'm going to run by and get them and see what's going on at the house."

"Maybe Kira is there," Jonah said, hopeful.

"And how would that have happened?" Noah asked, waving at the car.

Jonah shrugged. "What else would keep mom from picking up the boys? She'd never leave them waiting."

"That's exactly my thought. But Kira would never leave the kids waiting on pickup either. Which is why I'm scared."

With that, Noah went to his truck and climbed in, suddenly looking much older than his years. Jonah watched him go and felt ashamed that he couldn't do something—anything—to put everything right again.

But damned if he wasn't going to try.

Chapter Seven

A loud noise awakened Jules and she opened her eyes. It took her more effort than usual, but she finally sat up. When she looked at the clock on the kitchen wall, she felt a moment of panic.

Three o'clock!

She was late to get the boys was her first clear thought. The second was that this was another moment of clarity and she needed to hold on to it this time. There was something going on with her and it wasn't normal. Actually, it was downright terrifying.

Then she remembered.

Kira.

Her first attempt to get up didn't connect. Nothing moved. But finally, she struggled to her feet.

When she looked at the clock again, it was three forty-five. Where had the last forty-five minutes gone?

Suddenly, the front door flew open and she startled, catching her breath. When she saw Noah come through it, relief flooded through her system.

Behind him, her grandsons, Micah and Lukas, shoved at each other, trying to be the first to get to her.

"Nana, Micah punched me," Lukas said.

"I did not," Micah replied.

"Jules, what's going on? Why didn't you get the

boys?" Noah said, kneeling in front of her. When she didn't answer, he looked around the room. "Where's Gemma?"

"Wwwhhhhhhrrrr," she said, cringing when she heard her words.

Noah stood. "Boys! On the couch. Now. Don't move until I tell you."

Jules watched as he ran out of the room and down the hallway. She felt as though he, and the boys, were moving in slow motion.

Quickly Noah came back into view, holding Gemma, who was covered in something white and foamy.

"Kkkkkk," Jules mumbled. She needed to know if they had found her.

Noah grabbed a dish towel and sat Gemma down between the boys on the couch. "Clean her up. Your nana is sick, and I need to make some phone calls."

The tone he used made it clear to the boys that something was wrong. They didn't make a peep as they began to wipe the shaving foam from Gemma's surprised face.

Noah pulled his phone from his pocket. His next words shocked Jules to her core.

"Please send help. I think my wife is having a stroke."

Chapter Eight

Jonah slapped at the mosquitos buzzing around his ear as he struggled through the wild tangle of brambles and weeds back up to the trail. He thought he'd seen a sliver of color and had braved the wild overgrown wall of thorns to check it out. Once he got into it, though, he saw that it was only a random tiny yellow flower fighting thorns for its share of oxygen.

He backed out, carefully retracing where he'd broken through.

It was hot and humid, and his face and wrists stung; the sweat making the painful briar cuts burn like fire. But who was he to gripe about a few scratches when his sister was out there somewhere, possibly mangled, fighting to survive?

A sudden crack rang out and Jonah hit the ground and covered his head, his soldier's instincts kicking in before he realized it was nothing but a large tree limb breaking away from a trunk deep within the jungle. He jumped up, looking around to be sure no one saw his display of cowardice.

Once back to the trailhead, he made his way to his truck, opened the door, and pulled his hydro flask out. He took a long swig of water, swished it around in his mouth, then spit it out.

He wished he could go back to the Sunday a few years earlier when Kira told the family she and Michael were leaving Lahaina and moving to the outskirts of Makawao Town in the upcountry. He would've talked her out of it so that she would never have chosen the Makawao Reserve as a place to run off her stress.

At the time, Jonah understood. They were tired of the Lahaina tourist parade bustling day in and day out. The restaurants were always packed. You could never find parking. And pedestrians were everywhere, always in the way when you needed to be somewhere on time.

Jonah counted himself lucky that he and Quinn lived and worked up in Hana, a place that had an abundance of peace and quiet. He still kept his simple cabin on the premises of the inn. It was important for him to be there full-time now that Quinn and Liam had moved into their new home. Of course, she'd hired an inn manager, but even she had to go home sometimes too.

Once the day unfolded and everyone was checked in or checked out, his little place on the property was the picture of peaceful.

Makawao also had that feel of seclusion. With its wooden storefronts and leftover hitching posts, it held the charm of an old rustic frontier town. Other than a spectacular view of the ocean below, there was no access to beaches which meant no surfing or snorkeling to bring in anyone looking for a secret spot. And as far as Jonah knew, there wasn't a single souvenir shop like the ones that lined the streets of Paia.

What Makawao did have was a rich history that many visitors knew nothing about. It was home to the first Hawaiian cowboys—or Paniolo, as they were called— who were invited to the area from Mexico. They'd been recruited to teach the Maui farmers how to manage the wild cattle bred from a steer that had been brought to the island as a gift to the king.

Jonah's phone rang, jolting him back to the reality of the situation.

"Dad?" he answered.

"Jonah, listen to me. An ambulance is on its way here. I think your mom might be having a stroke."

Jonah stopped mid-stride, halfway to his truck.

"Jonah?"

"I'm here," he said, finding his voice. "Tell me what to do. Where will they take her? What about the kids? Is she conscious?"

The questions he belted out were nothing compared to what was swirling around in his head. Jonah felt the rug pulling out from under him. His mom never faltered. It was unfathomable.

"Yes, she's conscious but she's having trouble talking. Her movements are weird too. Has there been any sign of Kira?"

"No. I've searched every path for a few miles, Dad. If she's in there, she's way off trail."

"Okay, Jonah. I want you to stay there. There're only a few more hours of daylight and we need to escalate this. Call your grandmother and have her tell that detective that if his team doesn't start a search, they'd better look for a replacement for her annual donation. But do not, and I repeat, *do not* tell Helen about your mom. Right now, your mom doesn't need that."

Jonah rubbed his hand over his eyes. He was glad no one was there to see him. He might just lose it. Suddenly he felt like a teenager again.

"Dad, I'm scared."

"I am too, but everything is going to be fine. Don't come to the hospital because your mom would kill us both if we left there without finding Kira. You take care of that and I got Mom. Okay?"

Jonah nodded, his voice thick with tears.

"You hear me?" Noah said.

He cleared his throat. "Yes, don't worry about this. I got it. I'll get Grandmother involved so we can get an official search started. What about the kids?"

"Call Michael for me as soon as we hang up. Tell him to come straight here when he gets the message. I've called the neighbor to come over until he can pick up the boys. Quinn's arranging a sitter to get Gemma so she can meet me at the hospital. I want you to call Lani and tell her I said she's your co-captain. Now I gotta go, son."

"Okay, Dad. Please call me as soon as Mom gets admitted."

"I will. And Jonah, keep me updated."

Jonah nodded again, this time so choked up he was completely unable to respond. But he didn't have to because with that, the call disconnected.

There was no time to wish for his private little cabin at the Hana Hamoa and the refuge it brought him. He was about to face some of his biggest anxiety triggers.

People. Responsibility. Stress.

And his dad was depending on him.

Usually, the women in the family were the leaders of the pack. He and his dad just followed instructions. Most of the time, anyway. But that wasn't going to happen here. He and his dad both knew that Lani was going to be just about falling apart not only about Kira, but now about their mother.

He gave himself all of thirty seconds to clear the tears from his throat before he dialed his grandmother.

Fortunately, she was a practical, no-nonsense kind of woman. She didn't need a lot of talk before they got to the point and she hung up ready to make her own calls.

Jonah felt a little guilty about it. His mother hated

to use the family name and prestige to call in favors. Being born a Rocha had caused her nothing but pain and once rid of it, she never again claimed the name. But he hoped she'd understand this time, as it might mean the difference of life or death for Kira. Either way, Helen was a bulldozer and he'd started her ignition and put her in gear.

Then he took a deep breath and called Kim.

"Why haven't you answered your phone?" she demanded, having picked up on the first ring.

"Kim, listen, an ambulance is taking my mom to the hospital. Are you there today?"

Her voice changed immediately. "Yes, I just got here. What's wrong?"

"Maybe a stroke. Not sure."

For the first time, he considered what a benefit it was that his girlfriend was in the medical field and spent a lot of time at that hospital. She could be his eyes and ears while he worked on finding Kira.

"Oh, Jonah, I'm sorry. Are you on your way, too?"

"No. To top things off on today's shitshow, we can't find Kira. She didn't show up for work and her car is parked here at the Makawao Reserve. Her purse and phone are locked inside."

"That's unusual, isn't it?" she asked.

"Yeah, it is. Hey, I need to go. I've got more calls to make to get some help finding Kira."

"Okay. I'll find out where your mom is and what's going on once she's admitted. I'll send you a text when I can. Be careful, Jonah."

"Thanks. Bye."

Next, he called Lani and explained to her that no, he didn't believe that Kira was pulling any kind of attention-getting stunt. He felt in his gut that something was very wrong.

"And Lani, there's more," he said gently.

"What? Tell me."

"Dad called and he thinks Mom is having a stroke. An ambulance is en route to the house."

Just as predicted, Lani broke into sobs.

"What the hell is this day?" she got out between breaths.

"Look, everything is falling apart, but you can't, Lani. I need you. You and I need to find Kira. Stop crying and get your ass up here now. I'm not leaving this up to Maui PD. Bring your laptop, too."

She hung up without saying another word.

Jonah knew his sister would be there quicker than humanly possible. Because when it came down to it, he and his sisters showed up for each other and always would.

Chapter Nine

Jules could still hear everything going on around her when the ambulance pulled up to the emergency room doors. The ride over had been chaotic and terrifying, with the screaming sirens sending daggers through her head and the constant swerving and braking making her nauseous.

The emergency technician had stayed busy, hovering over her, poking, prodding, and doing whatever it was that his protocol called for.

Noah held her hand the whole way, sometimes talking to her and other times praying under his breath. More than anything, Jules hated that she was causing him so much anxiety and she wished she could reassure him, but she thought if she tried to speak and her words were still garbled, it would only scare him more.

She remained silent.

When the door opened, the chaos intensified times a hundred. Jules kept her eyes closed because the lights were painful, and her vision was acting up. It felt as though a shade had been pulled down over her left eye even when it was open—a very baffling feeling that she was trying to avoid.

"Kim," she heard Noah say. "I'm glad you're here."

"Jonah called me. I'm going to stay with you if you

don't mind," she replied.

"We couldn't possibly ask that of you. Let's save your expertise in case they start throwing out words we don't understand," Noah replied.

They talked more as Jules was being wheeled down the hall, but their voices were lost in the din of others. She heard someone calling out her status and ordering a CT scan stat. Jules couldn't remember if that test was the one that would put her in a tunnel-like machine, but she hoped it was because at least in there, everything else would be drowned out.

She was wheeled into a stall and she opened her eyes a crack, just enough to see a doctor in a white coat step in and quickly pull the curtain shut behind him. A nurse slipped through and slapped a blood pressure cuff on her arm.

Noah answered the questions related to her history and how he'd found her. He affirmed that she didn't suffer from diabetes or high blood pressure. She'd never had issues with her heart. The only medication she was on was something to help her sleep, as she had trouble shutting off all the thoughts in her head of things she needed to do. He couldn't remember the name of the drug.

"Trrddddnnnnnn," she mumbled the name of it, cringing when it sounded so foreign in her ears. That is not what she meant to say.

The doctor immediately began her preliminary neurological test, urging Jules to open her eyes.

"Smile for me," he said.

She tried.

"I want you to repeat after me: the snow in the fields is white."

She tried but her words came out sounding like a butchered attempt at a foreign language. Her mouth was not saying what her brain told it to and that was terrifying in a way that Jules had never known.

When she looked at Noah, the distress on his face made her feel guilty. She stopped trying.

"Close your eyes and extend both your arms straight out, palms out, and hold it for ten seconds," the doctor said.

Jules slowly pulled her arms up, struggling with the left one. It was being stubborn again. It felt like a wayward child, but she finally managed to lift it. She couldn't hold it for the ten second countdown, though.

"Mrs. Monroe, the probability is high that you are indeed having or have had a stroke. Things are going to start moving really quickly now because we need to know what we're dealing with. And if what I suspect is true, then the goal is to restore blood flow to the affected areas as soon as possible. The more brain cells I can save, the better your chances for a full recovery."

Jules nodded at the terrifying words then looked at Noah.

He was crying. She'd only ever seen him cry one other time.

She wanted so badly to tell him not to worry, that other than her headache, she wasn't in any pain. She locked eyes with him as best she could, and he leaned down and kissed her forehead.

The curtain opened, and Quinn stepped through.

"Mom, are you okay?" she asked. "Talk to us.'

Jules didn't answer. She was afraid of what her words would do.

"They suspect a stroke and are about to take her for a scan," Kim said.

"A stroke?" Quinn asked, flabbergasted. "Mom is healthy! How is it possible she could be having a stroke?"

"More than eighty percent of strokes are caused by blood clots," the doctor said. "Also, some patients have defects in their blood vessels that have been there since birth, little ticking time bombs. Or stress is a well-known trigger. Has your mother been under a lot of stress lately?"

Jules pictured Kira's face and remembered the urgent call from Jonah.

Noah nodded. "This morning especially. We're having a family issue."

The doctor continued. "I'm sorry. But speaking of family, the cause could also just be genetic. Do you know of anyone in her family who has had a stroke?"

Her father—she wanted to say. She'd completely forgotten about his death after a series of strokes. It was so long ago she barely even thought of him any longer. Noah probably didn't remember, and Quinn had never asked.

The doctor didn't wait any longer for them to answer. "Mr. Monroe, I'll come find you as soon as her test results are in," she said, then left.

The nurse pulled the sheet up to Jules's neck. "I want you to keep your arms and legs in, sweetheart. I'm not going to wait an eternity for transport to come down here, so you and I are going for a ride. Family, please go out to the waiting area and I'll send someone to get you and bring you to her room once we place her."

Jules felt panicked. Here was the moment. They were taking her away from Noah. What if she never saw him again?

Her throat closed up, already thick with tears. She held her good arm out and he clasped her hand, then bent over her.

"Jules, no matter what, *you fight*," he said. "I mean it. You hear me? You fight like you've never fought before.

I need you."

She knew that was the truest statement he'd ever made. They needed each other. They always had. Their relationship was like none she could've ever imagined, and she knew it was a once-in-a-lifetime kind of love. She didn't fear death, not really, but she did fear what would happen to Noah if he had to face life without her.

He stepped back and let Quinn get closer. She leaned down and placed a kiss on her mother's cheek, her tears splashing against Jules's skin.

"I love you, Mom. Be strong," she whispered hoarsely.

Her words moved Jules more than she could say. Jules had three daughters and she loved them all dearly. But this one—this daughter of hers who found her way back home—gave her such an unexpected gift.

Jules tried to smile at her. They had so much more to learn about each other. They'd already lost three decades, and she wouldn't allow herself to be deprived of any more time.

The nurse unlocked the brakes on the bed and wheeled Jules out from behind the curtain. Jules kept her eyes locked with Noah's as long as she could, and just before they turned the corner, he blew her a silent kiss, sending her his heart to hold on to for comfort.

"If you're wondering about a CT scan, it's just a big loud machine that will take some good photos for us," the nurse explained. "I'll get you to lay down on a table and when I tell you to, you'll hold your breath and not swallow for a few seconds. It's easy and I'll have you back to your handsome husband in no time at all."

The nurse could've been a professional race car driver in a previous life because seconds after she uttered those words, Jules swore she took the corners at thirty miles an hour. She felt like she was on a roller coaster ride that wouldn't end as they took a labyrinth of halls, with the nurse yelling for a wide berth when they approached other staff or visitors.

Finally, she was wheeled through some double doors and the nurse slowed her to a crawl, then stopped the bed from rolling and locked the wheels.

"Mrs. Monroe, we're here. Open your eyes and I'll help you sit, then we'll just slide onto the table and lie back down."

Jules opened her eyes and immediately closed them again. The lights were brutal to her pounding headache. But dutiful as always, she strained and opened them again.

The nurse took her hand and began to pull her up to a sitting position. About halfway up, it was lights out.

But this time, Jules's eyes were open.

She saw nothing. Heard nothing.

Other than a sudden whoosh.

Chapter Ten

Jonah took a look around him, astonished at how fast the once bare, quiet parking lot had become a nightmarish scene of fire trucks, police cars, and chaos. Whatever his grandmother had said to the task force, it had spurred them into motion. Unfortunately, that meant he'd been questioned by no less than three more officers or detectives, whatever they were, about the last time he'd seen Kira.

What was she wearing?

What was her mood?

Did she and her husband have marital problems?

Does she have a boyfriend?

Do you and your sister get along?

The questions went from standard to ridiculous and the only new thing that resulted from the interrogation was that he remembered Kira said she had to go by the post office when she left the restaurant. He bit his lip when he looked at the time. They had less than three hours until dark. He wanted to scream into the forest, demanding Kira to answer. But he'd already done that on his solo walks back and forth from his truck down the paths. He felt hoarse and parched now, and so damn frustrated.

He had to give the fire department credit, though.

They'd already sent in a small search and rescue team to get a head start. Now the captain was organizing another but giving them strict instructions to be out of there before sundown.

"Jonah."

He turned, facing Lani. She had stepped into take-charge mode and he was grateful. Too many people were coming to him for questions and instructions, and he felt the walls closing in on him.

"What?"

"I'm not convinced that she's in there," Lani said. "The police aren't either, judging by the way they're acting."

"I believe she is," he answered quietly.

"Well, it appears to me there are two investigations going. One pointed at the forest and the other at the possibility that she ran away or has been abducted."

"And those are possibilities that I won't discard," he replied, fear rippling cold down his spine. "But I still feel like we need to comb every inch of that forest to be sure."

Lani leaned in and lowered her voice. "I also think they suspect you know more than you do since you were supposedly the last one to see her. Also, they're raking Michael over the coals. I kind of feel sorry for him."

Jonah shrugged. "He can handle it. If he knows something, he needs to tell them. Tell us. If not, then he needs to treat this like a natural part of the investigation."

Michael had gotten all the messages as soon as he pulled in closer to shore. After getting the boys situated, he'd come straight to the reserve. Jonah had kept an eye on him since he'd arrived, gauging his demeanor. Michael was surprisingly calm. He wasn't usually so reserved in his emotions, always rising to anger quickly. Jonah half expected him to be more dramatic about his missing wife, but his lack of expression was making him look suspicious.

But who was Jonah to judge how one should act when their partner was in danger? Kira was his sister—maybe people thought he should be more distraught too. However, anyone who knew him knew he always kept his feelings close to his chest. That was just his way.

"Excuse me, are you the family of Kira Lambert, the missing woman?"

Jonah and Lani turned to find an older man staring up at them through wired spectacles. He held a phone in his hand, pointed their way as though he were recording them.

"Yes, why?" Jonah was tired of people approaching him just to be of no help.

"I'm Simon Lang, freelance reporter. Can you answer a few questions?" The tone of his inquiry didn't sound polite. More like entitled.

"No," both Jonah and Lani said at the same time.

The reporter paused, his eyes narrowing.

"Then I'll just run with what I have," he said challengingly. He stared at Jonah. "By the way, I covered Nama's story of being swept out to sea and disappearing several decades ago. You were just a boy, but weren't you also the last one to have seen her before her disappearance? That's going to make quite a hook. What are the odds of another member of your family disappearing into thin air with you in the hot seat yet again?"

Jonah felt Lani's hand come down to grip his arm, warning him not to react. His jaw ticked and was so tense it felt like it would snap.

"No comment," he said.

Michael took the opportunity to walk away, anger showing in the strength of his steps. Jonah wanted to follow.

"Mister Lang," Lani said. "Please—this is hard enough. My sister might be found any moment. There's a team in there now. Can you please just hold the dramatic scoop for a while?"

Jonah squelched the urge to punch the guy in the throat. But one, the man was a few years older than Jonah's dad and that made him off limits, and two, Jonah didn't need to be escorted to jail when he had one directive—to find his sister.

"I'll make you a deal," Lang said. "I don't want to hurt your family. I really don't. But I've been following all of you for years. Since your first tragedy. Consider me captivated and invested. I *will* be following up and I *would* like to give you the opportunity to tell your side, *Jonah*."

Jonah didn't answer.

Lani turned her back on him. "You *may* leave us alone now since you can see we have important things to do. I'd thank you for your concern in helping find my sister, but…"

Lang took the blow without the slightest reaction and walked away, a smug smirk across his face.

"Shake it off, brah," Lani said. "We already know it's going to get dirty. No use fighting it anymore. We have to focus on Kira. But at least we have a reprieve from the media circus that's sure to be coming."

She was right. The world was always ready to dig for dirt, to stir up rumors and untruths just to feel like someone had it worse than they did. They'd keep searching for any and every angle to make the story appear juicier than it really was.

Hell, Jonah knew his background would most likely be pulled—his misdemeanor arrests and past history of drug use was never going to stay in the rearview mirror. It would be fodder for however the media wanted to spin the story. It didn't matter that he'd been clean for more than five years and planned to never look at a drink or a pill again. If he could take it back and erase all the pain he'd caused, he would.

But he couldn't. It would forever be a stain on his reputation. And his conscience.

Once an addict, always an addict.

Isn't that what they say?

He felt nauseous. This was why he preferred not to be around people.

Lani read his mind because she put her arm around him and squeezed. "Just shut everyone out for a little while. Except me, creep."

She joked, but her words grounded him.

"And come on, Maggie and Colby are here. Quinn called them and asked them to come. They want to do something to help."

Maggie was Quinn's best friend, and Colby was her partner. Over the last two years, they'd become like family and Jonah was glad they'd come. He needed help and action, not accusations.

Lani led him to where they stood, talking to a small group of locals about the trail loops and severity of different ones. Their dog, Woodrow, sat obediently at Maggie's feet.

"Jonah," Maggie said, "We're here and we want to help. Tell us what to do."

Colby reached over and pumped his hand, then patted him on the back as they embraced.

"Thanks for coming," Jonah said, feeling misty-eyed. "Where's Charlie?"

"He's with Rosa," Maggie said. "He has no idea what's going on. She promised him a strawberry smoothie in a big cup if he didn't give her any trouble for the evening."

Jonah smiled at that. The boy was a great negotiator. Smoothies on the island weren't cheap.

A phone rang and both Jonah and Lani reached for theirs.

"It's mine," she said, flipping her case open and holding it to her ear. She turned away to take it, leaving Jonah with Maggie and Colby.

"Anyway," Jonah continued, "A friend I went to school with is on the police force and since I know the guys on the case won't tell us anything, I'll put a message out to him to see what angles they're exploring."

Lani shrieked and dropped her phone. Jonah rushed to her side and she fell into his arms, sobbing uncontrollably. He couldn't let her go or she'd fall to the ground.

Maggie picked up the phone and turned away, resuming the conversation. When she ended the call, she turned back, and Jonah could see her face had gone pale.

"That was Quinn," she said. "Your mom had a massive stroke at the hospital as they were preparing her for a test. They've put her in a drug-induced coma."

Jonah stared at Maggie, silently pleading for her to take it back. He couldn't say a word, even if they could have heard him over Lani's ragged cries. Suddenly he wasn't sure who was holding who up. He felt his world crashing in around him and he locked eyes with Colby.

Colby shook his head, solemn. Jonah could feel the message he was sending over Maggie's head.

And he listened.

He could fall apart later.

After he found Kira.

"It's going to be okay," he whispered as he stroked Lani's hair. He'd found his voice again and this time nothing was going to take it away. There was no doubt in him that his mom would want him to stay and not give up until he found Kira, her youngest child.

So that's what he would do.

Jonah was ready for battle. He wouldn't let the universe come for his family again. It was time to flex and send the message that no matter what it threw in their path, they were stronger, and they would beat it.

He handed Lani over to Maggie and turned around, striding toward the small pods of authorities. If they thought they were going to push him to the sidelines and make him wait for answers, they were on the wrong damn island.

Chapter Eleven

Jules had no concept of time as she drifted quietly in the dark, the silence a comfortable cloak of security around her. If she were more alert, she would know that her mind was empty. It no longer sorted through an endless reel of thoughts, plans, and memories.

Instead, she knew not what was missing, and held no expectations of what was to come.

She just was.

And it was fine.

She couldn't think of a better way to describe that she was not there, yet she was, in some sort of ethereal way.

It felt…. comforting.

Was this death?

She didn't know, but she felt no pain and no urgency to be anywhere else.

She waited quietly, for what she wasn't sure, but somehow, she knew there was more to come. Something amazing.

Tiny particles of sparkly light surrounded her, moving in waves as though alive, and Jules felt as though she knew them and they her. She had never before felt so relaxed or so welcome.

After a bit—a long time or only a millisecond, she didn't know—a tiny pinprick of light pierced the soothing blackness beneath her. In the light, just below but too far to measure, she could see her own body barely visible through a hazy layer of energy.

It lay on a hospital bed, hooked to a lot of tubes and wires. And it wasn't moving. The pinprick eventually grew to the size of a postage stamp, then a dinner plate; however, Jules moved no closer to the body.

She studied it, thoughtful and sympathetic, sorry she had been so judgmental over the years about its flaws and shortcomings. For all intents and purposes, the body had fought for her, she knew this now. It had done its best to contain her spirit and do her proud for nearly six decades, yet Jules had never shown it any sort of gratitude and that made her sad.

Suddenly the air around her felt different.

Heavier.

Voices were coming to her, but so faint that she couldn't make them out. One of them called deeper to her than the others, feeling more familiar. It increased in volume—just a tiny bit—but she could feel the longing in it.

Slowly, she began to move toward her body, the only tangible thing she could almost see. Her descent was not by choice. She wanted to stay with the glistening particles—yearned to see what their silent promise of acceptance would mean. However, as though an invisible piece of twine pulled her in, she suddenly felt herself sucked through what felt like a vortex of pain until it stopped suddenly.

And she could see nothing.

The loud rhythmic sound of the machine clasped over her face made a clinical background racket.

Jules wanted to pull it free and let herself go back to the peaceful silence. To the tiny lights of energy.

Please, take me back, she pleaded.

Then she heard his voice again. Faintly. Oh, so very faintly.

Fight, Jules. Stay with me, he said.

She knew it now. So familiar.

It was Noah. Her love. Her soulmate. His voice passionately held her back from embracing whatever was next for her. His hold on her was tenuous but still there. She didn't want to stay or return. She wasn't even sure where she was. All she could think of was the way she'd felt just a short time earlier. Free. Another voice cut through the dark fog. It was young, feminine.

She didn't recognize it.

"My studies show that patients fight harder for their lives if they know exactly what is going on," she said.

Yet another female was crying. Jules heard her muffled, pitiful sobs.

A third, more authoritative voice broke in. "That's enough. From here on out when you are near the patient, no tears and all positive energy. Want to cry? Take it outside. Want to talk about what could happen or might come to be? Swallow it and instead, remind her that she *will* recover, no matter what we find. The alternative doesn't need to be discussed in here."

That woman was tending to her, doing things to her body that Jules couldn't quite feel, though she knew something was happening. Finally, it stopped, and her tone of authority carried as she was leaving the room.

"She's stable for the moment. But you need to wrap this up and let her rest," she said, then the voice was gone, and the room was quiet again.

"Can she hear us?" Noah asked, breaking in.

The first female answered. "Personally, I think she can. You've got a good nurse there but beware, later you'll probably have some medical staff who will tell you that Jules is unaware of anything that is happening. This is my field of study and I can tell you that there have been many cases of people coming out of a coma who claim they could hear what was going on around them."

"I hope she can," the other female said.

"My advice is to talk to her. It won't hurt anything, and you might get through enough for something to kick in and make her hold on. She has a very fragile grasp on life right now. We want to bring her back."

"I don't even know what to say." That was Noah again. Her rock.

He usually didn't need to plan what he said to her. He never had. They could drive for hours in the car, comfortable in their compatible silence as they took in the scenery around them. Words came easily between them but were never needed.

"Dad, please, don't cry," a female said.

Jules knew her voice but couldn't quite pinpoint who she was.

But her heart broke for Noah. Emotion flooded her senses. She tried to speak but could not. She told her hand to move, and it refused. She begged her eyes to blink but they ignored her.

All she could do was lie there, making him suffer through his anguish.

"Let me start," the feminine voice said. "Jules, this is Kim. You are in the neuro-ICU of Maui Medical. You've suffered a severe hemorrhagic stroke. The bleed is deep in the left side of your brain in a place called the thalamus and it cannot be operated on. They've inserted a drain into your head to relieve the pressure and drain some of the blood. You're on a ventilator, so you cannot talk, and you've been sedated to keep your blood pressure and other vitals controlled."

Jules heard every word but other than her sympathy for Noah, the given status didn't alarm her. She really didn't even understand it.

"Jules," Noah said, his voice thick with emotion. "I'm here, babe. I'm not going anywhere. Quinn is here too. We'll stay with you so you won't be alone. You let your brain rest so you can come back to us. But don't slip too far away, okay?"

She didn't know if she could promise him that she wouldn't slip away. She was waiting to go back to that ethereal, peaceful state. She longed to be untethered.

It was all she could think about, and she wasn't sure she'd remember how to return to the place she'd left.

Day Two

Chapter Twelve

Jonah crawled out of the cab of his truck before daybreak, finally giving up the longing for a few hours of sleep. Between racking his brain, trying to remember every word that Kira had said at breakfast the day before, and his worry over where she had spent the night, as well as over his mom's condition, sleep definitely did not happen.

He was also still fuming that the search had been called to a halt at sunset.

SAR—the Maui search and rescue team that had responded—had barely had time to check out a few trails before dark descended on them. Despite Jonah's pleas to keep going, to use headlamps if needed, they'd refused to jeopardize their volunteers.

Not only did they not go out, but they'd roped off the trailhead and asked that no one else enter the reserve until morning. Jonah was frustrated, but he could understand. No one wanted any evidence Kira may have left behind to be damaged or kicked out of sight.

As for Maui PD, Jonah still didn't feel they were taking it seriously enough. They kept circling back to the conclusion that she may have disappeared voluntarily.

Jonah had never known his sister to leave her phone and keys behind, though he wasn't intimately familiar with all her habits. But it just felt wrong.

He'd given the MPD full permission to do a search of the interior of her vehicle, but other than her hydro flask full of water and her wallet, they found nothing else useful.

The fact that her water had been left in her car had bothered him all night. She could be out there thirsty. Hurt. Trapped.

Methodically, he went through the scenarios of what could've happened to prevent her from returning to her car.

She'd gotten lost would obviously be the big one. That would entertain the thought that she'd gone off trail for some reason. Perhaps someone had chased her off trail? Or she'd needed to relieve herself and gotten turned around? The reserve was a tangled jungle, and someone could very easily walk three feet off the trail and not be able to find their way back to it.

But then, why wouldn't she call out? Or why hadn't they found any evidence of her out there?

Then there were the wild hogs.

The jungle was full of them and if Kira had happened upon a pack with a litter of babies, there could've been trouble. The hogs could run pretty damn fast, from what he remembered of an experience he'd had as a teenager. He'd been lucky to avoid being impaled.

Then again, there'd be some sign of a scramble. Overturned earth. Broken branches.

And then there was the other scenario, which he could barely stand to fathom. That some monster had taken her, who knows where, and was torturing her even now. As kids, he had always reassured her that there was no such thing as monsters and that he would always keep her safe; he couldn't handle the possibility that he was wrong.

Many times throughout the night, he'd had to revert his thoughts back to positive ones. He didn't want to send any negative energy into the universe on her name.

To keep busy, he'd texted Quinn and asked for updates on their mom, but so far there were no changes. He hadn't even tried to call his dad, as Kim had told him that he'd been nearly inconsolable and was just barely keeping it together. Jonah didn't want him to have to talk through his agony.

Kim—she was a godsend, he had to admit, and his only lifeline to what was going on with his mom, boiling down the medical terms and her status so he could understand it all. He hadn't even had to ask her to stay there. It was unspoken, though she'd already been at the hospital more than twenty-four hours.

Who would've thought that bringing in a team to take care of their frustrating coqui frog invasion at the inn would have led to his first real relationship in years—and the best one he'd ever had?

At first, he was taken by Kim's adventurous side that led her into the jungle unafraid of anything, but then he discovered that she was also an intellectual on track to get a medical degree. And now, she was standing in for him in one of the most important roles of his life.

Jonah slammed his fist on the hood of his truck, his frustration escaping his normally calm demeanor. He felt guilty as hell for not being at his mom's side.

He walked to the trailhead and paused, throwing his head back.

"KIRA, I'M STILL HERE!" he bellowed out as loudly as possible.

Then again, for good measure.

At many points during the night, he'd played music as loud as he could with his truck windows down. Every hour he laid on his horn for as long as he could stand it.

If she was really out there, he hoped she could hear a wisp of the tunes or the horn blast to help bring her closer, or at least let her know she wasn't alone.

It was a lonely night. Jonah had sent Lani home to get some rest, as though that would happen. Michael had also gone home to take care of the boys. He was going to tell them that Kira had gone to the Big Island for a few days on business. Jonah didn't agree with lying to them but that wasn't his choice. At some point, if she wasn't found…well, he didn't even want to think about that possibility.

Memories of Kira plagued him throughout the night. He recalled her on her wedding day, beaming ear to ear out on the beach, oblivious to the scowl he wore because he wasn't quite fond of her partner choice. But she'd beamed even wider when he'd visited her in the hospital to meet his first nephew. To Jonah, Kira looked like a kid holding a baby. But she was a hell of a mother. Protective and caring, always wearing herself out for her family.

He thought of her as a kid, always trying to tag along with him more than she did with Lani. He knew why. He was gentler with her while their sister could be too tough, always bossing her around. Jonah sensed right away that Kira didn't have the same tough exterior as Lani. She was softer. More vulnerable. Because of that, he'd always gone above and beyond to protect her. And she knew he would. She bragged on her big brother all their lives, knowing he'd step up for her with one flick of her finger.

That's why now he felt so damn helpless. What if she was depending on him and he was failing her?

Jonah shook it off, not wanting to go there.

He stood completely still, listening. The sun was gradually rising and all around the reserve, birds and insects were making their morning racket. But he heard nothing else out of place. He stretched, trying to work out some of the kinks that had wrestled their way into his neck and back. What a long night, leading into what he assumed was going to be an even longer day.

The loud motor of a truck startled him, and he turned to see it pull in, park, and four men climb out. They were dressed for hiking and each carried a backpack.

It was the first team in from SAR and Jonah was thankful to see them arrive so early. Today was the big day, and they would be pulling out all the stops and sending in their best searchers, including some trained for rappelling the cliffs and sharp drop-offs.

The lead man approached him, and Jonah recognized him right away. It was Derek, a friend he'd met during his beach-living years.

Derek gave him a sympathetic grimace. "Dude, I had no idea it was your sister who's missing until this morning when I got a call that the other lead is sick. I'm so sorry."

Jonah held his hand out and Derek took it, shaking it eagerly. Jonah noticed he wore a bright yellow vest and all the other accessories a professional would don. He was clean, his hair shorter than Jonah remembered him wearing it too. The most glaring difference was that his friend was wearing shoes. Appropriate ones for hiking, at that.

"Thanks, man. But hey—look at you. Who would've thought that you'd clean up so well?"

Derek smiled. "Found myself a good girl and she got me walking the straight and narrow. I got a job down at the Toyota dealership detailing cars, but I try to give back to Maui by doing this. And you know how I used to like to disappear for a day on the trails. This service has allowed me to find my *Ho'ohana*."

"Yeah, I remember you disappearing until you'd come back down to the beaches looking for whoever was handing out hot dogs," Jonah teased, but inside he felt warm that his old friend was happy.

Ho'ohana was the Hawaiian value of worthwhile work, and many never found what made their heart sing. Derek was lucky he had kept searching for his purpose, because Jonah's *Ho'ohana* still remained elusive.

"But seriously. Good on you. I hope you can find her. They won't let me back in and I feel like I'm going to explode any minute."

"We're going to give it our best shot. Yesterday they did a loose grid with purposeful wandering but today we're going to tighten up and make sure we don't miss anything. And I need to get moving before the other team arrives and gives me hell for not having a base camp set up yet."

Jonah watched him walk away. He hoped that the many times he'd shared his resources with Derek years before would earn him some extra brownie points and send them into places a team might not venture. He didn't want a single stone left unturned.

A few more vehicles arrived, and Lani jumped out of one. She spotted Jonah and came straight at him, flinging herself into his arms.

"I'm not crying," she said, her tone angry.

"Okay…"

"I mean it. I am *not* going to cry. I'm going to be useful and keep myself together, and *we* are going to get this done."

He hugged her tighter. "Of course you are. I'd expect nothing less. Anything new to report on Mom?"

Lani let him go and stepped back. She shook her head, swallowing hard.

"No. I was just up there. The doctor hadn't been by

yet. But Kim said something that made sense and made us all feel better. She said that when injured, the brain has to rest. It might try to wake up for a moment or two, then rest again."

"Mom woke up?" he asked, hope surging through him.

"No, but Kim wants us to be prepared in case she does, and then falls back into the coma."

"Oh, got it. Are Dad and Quinn still there too?"

"Yes. Liam brought them breakfast this morning and he's also coming here later to see what he can do. He has to check with the inn manager and the chef, then get Gemma situated. Quinn is keeping Dad calm. During the night, they only let one person in at a time and he had a bit of an upset over that, but she got him to understand. Well, she and Kim."

Maggie and Colby approached, their arms laden with cases of bottled water. Their dog, Woodrow, trailed behind them.

"Thanks, guys," Jonah said. He led them to a spot in the parking lot that was the closest to the trailhead. It was about fifty feet from where Derek was setting up his tent. "I think we can set up here next to the rescue crew."

Derek came over and bent his head toward the three of them.

"Listen. I'm going to give you some advice throughout today, just because I've been through this several times in the past few years."

"I appreciate that," Jonah said.

"First thing, we might find Kira today. But if I were you all, just in case we don't, I'd go ahead and appoint someone as the family spokesperson. Things can get dicey and the last thing you want is to stand up there and lose your shit when trying to reach out to people through the media. No offense, but Jonah, I worry that you'd come off as angry. Maybe we should appoint your sister?"

"I think she'd get too emotional to stay on track," Jonah said, raising his eyebrows at Lani.

"You're right," Lani said. "It's hard for me to hide my feelings and I might give the searchers the idea that it's hopeless to keep looking."

Jonah looked at Maggie. "Can you be the family spokesperson to handle media?"

She looked hesitant at first, then nodded. "I guess I need to get over my fear of being in the spotlight sooner or later. So yes, I can do that."

"Perfect," said Lani.

Jonah knew that this was a lot to ask, but he didn't know who else to turn to, or who else his family could trust. Maggie had been stalked for years, and as a result, avoided being anywhere near the internet or in newspapers.

"Look, if you don't want—" he started.

She held up a hand. "No. I'm fine and that is all behind me. I want to do this. I have a background in PR too, so I'm the best choice. I'll set up a Facebook page and try to get traction there. The more people who know Kira is missing, the better. Maybe someone has seen her."

"Great idea," Derek said. "And I know dealing with social media comes with some issues and backlash, but it's important to get Kira's face out there to the public in case we don't find her in there," he said, motioning to the trailhead.

They all fell silent.

"Sorry," Derek said.

"We *will* find her," Jonah insisted.

"Right. That's what I'm here for. If she's out there, I'll find her," Derek agreed. "Now, I need to get over there and organize my team."

"Wait," Jonah said. He looked at Maggie and Lani. "If you two and Colby are going to stay here and try to spearhead things, I'd like to go in with Derek."

Derek shifted from foot to foot. He grimaced. "Ah... Not sure about that, man."

"If you won't take me in with you, I'll go alone."

Derek shrugged. "Fine. As long as you don't go rogue in there. You have to follow my directions, or I'll get my ass nailed to the wall when you screw something up."

"Deal," Jonah said, relief washing over him. It was getting crowded in the parking lot with other locals sniffing out what was going on and already a news van was setting up. Even after the long, quiet night he'd had, he didn't want to face the noise again.

"You're going to need some long pants and gloves, unless you want to get all itchy. We'll be going through a lot of saw grass. And since the ground is unlevel, bring trekking poles if you have them." Derek bumped him on the elbow. "But we'd better hurry before the search manager gets here. I need to brief my crew."

No gloves or poles, but Jonah didn't care. He followed Derek to the small group of six that had gathered. They all wore the same vests with emblems identifying themselves as SAR.

"This is Jonah, Kira's brother," Derek said. "He's got a lot of hiking experience, but no search and rescue. He's going to tag us and will stay with me."

The five guys and one woman nodded. Jonah appreciated that they were somber and serious. They looked like they meant business.

"Did everyone bring a compass, radio, and a charged cell phone?" Derek asked.

They all nodded.

"Show me the whistles."

They picked up the whistles hanging from their necks,

waved them and dropped them. Derek pulled a spare from his pocket and handed it to Jonah.

"Alright." Derek pulled a map from his backpack and unfolded it, lying it on the ground. They all squatted around it. "I've defined our search area and rated the zones by probability. First, we'll check the drops, drainages, and any hiding holes we can see from these trails." He traced a line with his finger. "When Team Two gets here, they'll take the offshoots from the main trail, some of which have a few steep drops. They've got a search dog, so they'll be going in further."

"That reminds me. Please pay attention to the waterfalls," Jonah said. "I could see her going off trail to find one, then maybe falling and getting hurt."

"Absolutely," Derek said. "We'll mark and report back every waterfall once we clear it. We have a few rappelers on our team for the real treacherous ones. We don't want anyone who's not qualified to take any chances."

He stood. "Make sure you take notes on anything you come across. Any likely clues, you know the drill: call it in. And that is the briefing. Any questions?"

When no one spoke up, Derek gestured to the trailhead.

"Kira was last seen nearly twenty-four hours ago. We need to find her fast, so let's do this."

Chapter Thirteen

Jules was shocked. She was still alive. Her body was no longer floating, light and free. Instead, it felt like a heavy lump of clay.

And pain. So much pain.

She tried but failed to shift to one side. She also tried and failed to open her eyes. Her joints ached and her muscles screamed for relief, but she could move nothing.

Her nirvana was gone.

In its place was pure hell.

The sounds around her and the feeling of being pinned to the bed amongst a spider web of tubes and wires were her first clues that she was still hospitalized. If those hadn't done it, then the frequent flashes of light that streamed through the tiniest crack of her eyelids and pummeled her brain would've made it apparent.

Next on the list of inhumane torture to endure was the nurse who had come through for the last several hours. She talked loudly, her voice harsh and intruding. Abrasive. Jules silently begged the woman to quiet herself, to be gentle. The words she spoke didn't make sense, the sounds and pronunciation of anything were like a stew of nonsensical noise.

When the nurse wasn't directly addressing Jules, she

made conversation with others in the hallway, the noise filtering in and settling around the room.

They talked.

And talked.

Then talked some more.

Jules felt left out. And she realized she was angry.

At herself because it was her own fault.

She'd asked the universe to untether her and let her join the energy that linked all things, so she could find her way back to Noah. Now she had to embrace the pain, physically and mentally, that came with returning. In the state of euphoria she'd left behind, all her bad memories and worries had ceased to exist, or at least ceased to matter. A part of her wanted that feeling back, but she couldn't just let go and leave all of them.

She thought of Kira. That was a tether of another sort. Her daughter was in serious danger. Jules could feel it in every fiber of her being. She had to find a way to let them know.

"Is she still sedated?" a voice asked.

Jules didn't know what the words meant but she liked the sound. It felt familiar. Masculine.

"No, the sedation has lifted. She's showing signs of agitation, but her pupils are not responding to light."

"This is day two. What do we do now?"

"Now we wait for the body to reabsorb the blood on her brain."

"Then she'll come out of it?"

Silence.

A loud sound. Like a door.

Hushed talk.

Then touch. Someone crawled into the bed with her.

Jules tried to lean away. Her body remained still.

Whoever it was felt soft. Feminine.

Maternal.

"Helen, do you think that's a good idea? What if you pull something out?"

"Shush. She needs to know that she's not alone."

"Well, if you're doing that, I'm going to go down for coffee and to call Jonah and get an update on Kira. Quinn, come on. You need a break, too."

The door opened and closed.

Then, quiet.

The woman breathed warmth against her neck.

Then a whisper.

Jules strained, trying to make out the words. Wishing she would talk slower. More clearly. *Was she saying anything about Kira? Had they found her?*

Then she felt it. A touch on her wrist, then up her arm. A slight butterfly feeling of swirls over and over. It was so comforting. The words continued and slowed to a pace that Jules could start to understand. She strained to hear something—anything about Kira.

"We didn't always have such a distance between us. At first you wanted to be near me all the time. Always touching. I know you don't remember, but you were my shadow and I adored having you underfoot."

That's exactly how Kira was when she was young, always clinging to Jules.

"Soon, though, you wanted freedom. From the time you could walk it was obvious that you craved it. But I didn't want you have to have it. I wanted to keep you tethered to me. Your brothers were wild, nearly uncontrollable, and I tried to keep their rebellion from transferring to you. And despite my efforts, it found you anyway. With a stronger, more sweeping force. Your brothers always came back to me. But you—once you found your legs, there was no stopping you."

Helen talked on, reminding Jules that she was needed by Noah and her children. She reminded Jules how strong she was, how she'd given birth to all of her children without the tempting allure of medication. How Kira had been her longest birth of all, and Jules refused to submit to the doctor's offer of something to cut the pain. She spoke of how Kira had been the child who brought the sun with her, making people smile wherever she went.

Kira, where are you?

Jules saw her daughter, just a child with long dark braids trailing behind her as she ran to catch up. Then Kira, bringing her a sun-bleached seahorse, cradling it close to her as she cried and begged for help to get it back to the deep water. She was her most intuitive child, the one with the most inquisitive questions coming from someone so young.

"Where do our spirits wait for our bodies to join them when we die?" she'd asked at only five years old.

How had she even known what a spirit was? And why was she more interested in that subject than the simple things that piqued most little girls?

Kira's spiritual awareness would only grow stronger as she aged, much more so than any of Jules's other children. It was something the two of them shared, a connection that bonded them further than Jules would've imagined was possible after the loss of her first daughter.

She saw Kira again. This time at her full age and in a sitting position, her head in her hands as her body shook with sobs. She looked drawn and exhausted. And so very lost.

Jules could feel her daughter's pain and desperation as though it were her own, but she couldn't discern where Kira was. Her vision didn't include the surroundings.

Where was she? Was she with someone? Someone dangerous?

"Don't give up," Jules thought, willing the message to reach Kira.

Jules wanted to go to her! She tried to raise up, to move her limbs, but nothing happened. Her fury at her own body raged around her, causing her pulse to race faster and faster until she hit a wall and it stopped.

She sank into the sweet oblivion that welcomed her once again.

Then she felt a jolt, and she opened her eyes and there he was.

Noah.

Jules followed Noah out of the surf and to the public outdoor shower. They propped their surfboards against the wall of the building, then washed the grit from their feet and legs, laughing as they kicked the cold water at each other. She had conquered a massive wave, and she still felt the adrenaline rushing through her. Her muscles quivered and her heart thumped rapidly in her chest.

She was glad he'd seen her do it too. Now he knew she was capable and not just some wide-eyed beach bunny with a good tan.

When he reached over to wipe sand from above her eyebrow, she felt it again. That surge of butterflies in her stomach. Euphoria rushed through her.

"Don't want that falling into your eyes," he said.

He was gentle. So very gentle.

The way he looked at her made her breathless, as though he believed she was the most beautiful girl in the world.

Jules was eighteen and she knew that indeed, she had looks that brought attention. But the kind from Noah were different.

Deeper.

He cared about her—but he didn't care that she was a Rocha.

She'd fallen for him hard. She forced herself to tell him that her family had a reputation around Maui. They were wealthy, but worse than that was the fact that some said their wealth had been gained dishonestly. She'd nearly choked on the words as she told the story, but she felt it important that he know who she was.

Noah said that the fact that it bothered her told him enough about her and her moral compass, and that she shouldn't be held accountable for someone else's misdeeds. Relief had flooded through her. For once, someone looked at her like she was her own person.

They finished at the spigot and picked up their surf-boards, then walked to the tent he had set up under the banyan trees. They propped the boards together against a tree trunk.

"I'll heat some hotdogs," he said. He laid out a towel on the ground, then pointed at it. "You rest."

She loved that about him. He was concerned about her and was the perfect gentleman. If he had a car, she could imagine he'd be the type to open the door for her. She settled onto the towel. His campsite was cozy, the majestic limbs around and over them providing a feeling of protection, as though the tree held them in its embrace.

He went into the tent for supplies, then returned and bent down to start a small fire. He took twigs from a pile to his right and stacked them.

Jules watched him, her arms wrapped around her legs and her chin on her knees. She never tired of looking at him—his blonde hair and blue eyes were exotic to her. The angles of his face strong and noble. His moves smooth and almost graceful.

"Tell me more about California," she said.

Noah had only been on the island a few weeks when he'd spotted her in the water, calling out to her that she looked like a mermaid. He'd stood on the sand, watching her until she came out and joined him on the beach.

Jules wasn't normally open to that kind of flirting. She wasn't a fan of pushy men, especially considering how her father and grandfather tried to bully her into being someone she wasn't. As had her brothers, in their own way. She loved them but they had treated her like she was a baby. They were always the ones going off on explorations, leaving Jules to make her own fun and interact with her imaginary playmates. They made her feel inferior, less deserving of the big life of adventure they lived.

Yes, she had a natural distrust of the male species, and her dating life, or lack thereof, had been a huge indicator of that. Most of the guys she'd gone to school with had only wanted one thing and jumping from girl to girl was their usual game. After she'd emerged from her ugly duckling stage, the surfers and the football players all vied for her, trying to woo her over to one side or the other.

Jules had refused them all. She wasn't going to be anyone's quickie. She didn't care if they thought she was weird for not having a boyfriend.

Something about Noah had pulled her in, as though it was a moment written in stone that she couldn't ignore. That had been the beginning of what she now hoped never ended.

He smiled. A small flame had started and before he spoke, he blew on it gently to coax the flames. Her stomach growled, anticipating food.

"Not a lot to tell. Did I mention there's too many people?"

She laughed. He actually had said that. Several times. The statement made sense because he had a very quiet nature about him, and she could imagine that being in the midst of hordes of people would be unsettling.

"Why did you choose Maui?" she asked.

"I came here once with my dad when I was twelve. I had been surfing the Cali beaches since I was four years old, but when I paddled into the waves from this beach, I felt like I'd come home. It was a surreal feeling, and I begged my dad to move us here."

"What did your mom say about it?"

"Mom didn't come on that trip. She said she had other things to do. Later, I found out that this was just a trial for me to be alone with my dad and see how he did with the sole responsibility. My mom left him a few months later, and then it was just the two of us."

Jules felt a wave of sadness.

"I fell in love with Maui. I told him as soon as I was eighteen, I was coming back here."

"And here you are," Jules said.

"Here I am." He winked at her.

"Now what?" she asked.

"Well, I'm going to have my own business. Just haven't quite figured out what it will be yet. I plan to make a good life here. I'm staying, but I won't be a beach bum for long."

Something in the way he said it made Jules believe with her whole heart that Noah would succeed. He had already proven he was a man of his word—following up on his pledge to return to Maui after six years of planning and saving for it.

"You've certainly got the chops to give some surfing lessons," Jules remarked. For not being an island boy, Noah looked like a pro out there. He had natural talent that she didn't see often.

"That's a great idea. And you're not so bad yourself. Maybe you could be my partner."

He wasn't smiling at her now. He was serious.

Jules found that she was nodding her head, agreeing to something she knew wouldn't go over well with her family. She didn't need to start a business, they'd say. She had everything she could desire at her fingertips. All she had to do to get it was behave and follow the plans laid out for her.

They thought they could dictate her future. Every damn step of it. Noah's offer was tempting, even if a little far-flung. Who was going to take lessons from them, as young as they were?

"Is that a yes?" Noah asked, his voice soft.

She could tell that he believed in his dream.

Believed in them.

"It's a yes," she whispered.

He came around the fire and pulled her up from her towel, straight into his arms. She was instantly warmed, the remnants of the sea water disappearing under his touch. He bent his head and gently kissed her.

Jules felt her soul burst with what she only hoped was pure, true love. His lips. They tasted so good. Salty and soft, all at once.

She wanted more. Much more.

Then a clatter of sound drew them apart. Everything went dark and she was suddenly alone. Alarmed and confused, she reached, trying to find Noah again, desperate to be back in his arms.

Helen sat in the small waiting room, absentmindedly

shredding a Kleenex over her lap. She'd seen the way that Noah had looked at her, his expression protective and guarded when he and Quinn had returned to the room and saw her painting swirls with her fingers over Jules's skin.

"What are you doing to her?" he'd asked.

"Nothing. Anyway, I think she might be waking up," Helen said, just before the blood pressure machine began to beep out an alarm and a nurse rushed into the room.

"I just talked to her the entire time you two were gone," Helen said.

The nurse read the numbers on the machine. "Her blood pressure spiked, but it's going down now."

"Something you said must've gotten through and upset her," Noah said. The way he looked at her, as though she'd done something wrong, struck Helen to the core.

She left the room and immediately went down the hall to the waiting room before he could ask her to leave. She'd only talked of good things—of Jonah and the girls and how Jules needed to come back to them.

Yet she left the room with a guilty conscience. *Had* she upset Jules?

The waiting room was eerily quiet.

Where were all the family members of the other patients?

Time passed painfully slowly staring at an empty room. It gave her too much time to think. She looked at her watch and thought of Cinder. The little bossy pants would be worried about her if she was away too much longer. But Helen didn't want to leave Jules. Even if she couldn't be in the room, at least she was only a short walk away.

She scooped up all the tissue and shoved it into her purse. Noah hadn't liked her crawling into the hospital bed. But why did he think that he had more right to Jules than she did?

Obviously, it was unusual for Helen to act in such an affectionate way, but she'd felt strongly that Jules needed to feel a mother's touch. She knew it looked weird, and yes, probably shockingly out of character, but Helen had felt an irresistible pull to be as close to her daughter as she could physically get. No matter that Jules was old enough to be a grandmother herself—she would always be Helen's youngest child.

It had been so long since she'd held Jules, and she couldn't resist having her close just for a moment.

Before she had to give her back over to Noah.

Helen had to admit, Noah had turned out to be a great husband and even better father. But as Jules's mother, she felt that her pain and worry over her daughter far magnified his.

She'd carried Jules for nine months. Nursed her and taught her to walk and talk. Rocked her to sleep and kissed her fingers and toes. Taught her to experience the world and everything in it.

Well, maybe that last part was something she couldn't take credit for. Jules had grown up with a streak of independence, and try as Helen might, she couldn't anchor her daughter to her. Jules had eventually wandered, starting the day she'd met her Noah on the beach.

Despite the battles that meeting Noah had prompted between her and her daughter, Helen had never stopped worrying over Jules, nor had she ever stopped loving her. She'd always wanted to protect her from the negative energy that their family name and the reputation of her grandfather's misdeeds had brought about. Many said their family name had a curse upon it, and when Helen put all the bad happenings together from years past, she truly believed it and didn't want it to touch the only daughter she had left.

Her boys didn't live on Maui any longer. They chose to take their lives to Oahu, a bigger island where the money flowed more easily. Maui was too small for their dreams, they'd said, as one after the other, they explained their plans to move away. Their absence left her with only Jules close by, which was ironic because in emotional distance, her daughter was the furthest away.

After Noah came into the picture, it only got worse. Jules had wanted nothing to do with her family name, their money, and especially hurtful, her mother.

Helen knew she'd made mistakes. Lots of them. But what mother hadn't?

"Would you like some coffee?" a young woman asked, breaking Helen out of her thoughts. "I just made a new pot."

The woman gestured toward a table holding coffee and condiments. Helen went over and made a cup—black, no frills—then returned to her chair. She was so cold that just holding the cup warmed her a little and she returned to her thoughts.

After so many years of turmoil, then came Jonah. When he was born, it changed things between her and Jules. Thankfully, her daughter decided her son needed to know more of his family, and she started coming around again.

Helen couldn't have been more ecstatic about the change of events. She vowed to be a different sort of grandmother than she was a mother, letting go of the constant urge to steer her children in the right direction and giving Jonah the freedom that she'd never let Jules have at such a young age.

She took Jonah on long walks, let him explore all their land, and even provided horse riding lessons. She was protective, because that was her nature, but the pressure to save him from the world was not hers. That belonged to his parents. All she had to do was focus on loving him.

Then their next child was born, a tiny girl named Nama. Noah and Jules married then, and surprisingly, accepted a gift of land from Helen. They built their own house and the visits still came, though much more sparingly since they were so busy, raising two children and running a business that was rapidly growing.

A shadow crossed her path and Helen looked up.

Noah was there and he sat down, his face frighteningly worried.

She felt her breath freeze in her chest. Please, God, no. Not her only daughter.

"Helen," he said. "I'm sorry. I don't want you to feel that you aren't wanted. I think Jules needs you too. It's going to take all of us to bring her back."

She couldn't speak, but she kept her chin up and her expression impassive.

"You can take the next shift," he said.

Chapter Fourteen

Jonah was hot and exhausted when he finally emerged out of the Makawao Reserve and headed to the parking lot, four-and-a half hours after going in. Despite what he considered a highly professional team of searchers, and looking under, over, and behind every rock, tree, and ravine in their outlined grid, they hadn't found a single piece of evidence that Kira had been in there.

Jonah wished again that someone would step up and offer the use of their helicopter. It was a shame that the search and rescue team didn't have its own. But Lani was still working on finding one.

In the meantime, they were knocking out the immediate area around the trailhead. Their SAR map was getting filled in, and they'd also checked most of the outlying trail systems. They'd even crossed three waterfalls off their list. Two divers had gone all the way to the bottom of the pools and thankfully came up empty, other than a few pair of sunglasses, a watch, and a surprisingly fancy engagement ring that would be posted on the SAR Facebook page to hopefully be reunited with its owner.

Jonah breathed a sigh of relief that at least some of the waterfalls were cleared. He knew that the falls could be dangerous, not only because of their height and slippery rocks, but because the pools below them held downed trees, old, barbed wire, and fishing line, not to mention that flash floods were possible.

As he'd moved with the others, his thoughts had bounced between the well-being of his sister and his mom. The last he'd heard from Kim was early that morning as she was headed home to get some sleep.

"We'll regroup after we all get some rest, and the other team comes out. There'll be a briefing before we start again," Derek said, then headed for his truck.

The parking lot was busy, with several search teams waiting for instructions and as well as most of the members of the Maui Fire Department milling about. Jonah wasn't really sure what they were doing. He knew another team was still in there, having entered from a different direction right after Derek's team, but by the look on everyone's faces, no one had found or heard anything.

The first person he locked eyes with was Lani, and she didn't appear to be in any better spirits either.

"Come here," she said, waving him over.

Maggie and Colby were still on site, and they looked away as he approached. Something was wrong.

Lani beckoned for him to follow and she led him to a corner just beyond the parked cars where they could be alone.

"They can only give us a 72-hour search window. Tomorrow is it," she said. "And Maui PD wants to get in your truck."

"My truck? Why?" He looked over to his vehicle and sure enough, there was yellow tape around it. "What the hell?"

"You were the last one to have seen Kira." Lani looked worried.

"What about Michael?"

"He didn't actually see her between when she left the house and came here. But yes, they've asked to search his car and the house too. If he doesn't cooperate, they're going to get a warrant. This is all so insane"

"Damn it," Jonah said. He was pissed. They were wasting good manpower going down the wrong roads. If Kira wasn't in the forest and someone *had* snatched her, it sure as hell wasn't him. And even though Michael could be an asshole at times, as far as Jonah could see, he loved Kira. He also loved his boys and he'd never want them to go without a mother.

Jonah's gut told him she was out there. Somewhere in that damn jungle.

"And before you ask, Mom's status is the same. Grandma said she noticed some movement, but the nurses say it's just natural reflexes."

"Probably a subconscious reflex of avoidance, if Grandma is in there talking to her," Jonah said. They all knew how much their mom struggled in her relationship with Helen.

"Quinn said Grandma crawled into the hospital bed with Mom."

Jonah raised his eyebrows, sure that the surprise was displayed on his face. Their grandmother wasn't the touchy-feely type. If Lani had told him she'd pointed at Jules, demanding her to awaken and sit up, that would be more believable.

But crawling into bed with her? That was *not* his grandmother.

He wondered if the stress was sending Helen over the edge.

Lani shifted slightly. "And she's been making calls to the mayor, insisting he up the resources to find Kira."

Jonah nodded. "Now that sounds like her. I'm going to take a break and go up to the hospital. Can you stay here?"

"Of course," she said.

They walked back to where Maggie and Colby were huddled.

"Thanks for being here all morning, guys," Jonah said. He bent down to squat in front of Woodrow, scratching him behind his ears.

"Too bad you aren't a tracking dog," he said. "But you're still a good boy."

Woodrow thumped his tail on the ground.

"Man, I'm sorry," Colby said, looking at his feet.

"Don't say that," Jonah said. "We're still going to find her."

"Yes," Maggie agreed. "We'll find her."

He looked up at them. "I don't want you guys to spend the entire day here. I know Charlie will be out of school in a couple hours."

Colby nodded and looked guilty. "He's got his first soccer game tonight. He's pretty stoked."

"Then you need to be there, buddy," Jonah said. "Tell him I wish I could be there too."

"I'll stay here with you, Lani," Maggie said. "Colby can take Charlie."

"No. You should both be there for his first game," Lani answered. "We've got two teams of search and rescue out there, and the MPD are determined to follow any leads outside of the jungle. There's not much you can do."

Jonah said, "But if you'll be here another hour or so, I'd like to run up to the hospital and see about Mom."

"Of course," both Colby and Maggie said at the same time.

Jonah kicked at the dirt. What if she woke when he was there and asked about Kira? And his dad—he'd be there too. Could he face him right now, with not one tiny clue as to where the hell Kira was?

"On second thought, I'll go tomorrow," he said. "I need to stay here today."

Lani bridged the distance between them and put her arm around his shoulder.

"Tomorrow will be fine."

Suddenly, they heard a ruckus and turned to see two volunteers talking to a SAR leader. He turned and waved them over.

Jonah trailed behind Lani.

"Could this belong to Kira?" the leader asked, holding out a sneaker, dirty white with a pink stripe. "They found it in a ravine."

Lani stared at it. "It looks about her size, but I don't think she has a pair like this. Let me send a photo to Michael and ask to be sure."

"Where the hell *is* he anyway? He should be here," Jonah said.

Lani took her phone from her pocket and dialed, then held it to her ear. They all heard the phone ring behind them.

"Hey," Michael called out. He had his phone in his hand and had seen it was Lani. He shoved it back in his pocket as he approached.

"Oh, we didn't know you were here," she said.

"I just got here. I've been at the house going through Kira's emails, looking for any clue that she had arranged to leave. Which, by the way, I didn't find a single thing." He held his hands up. "But before you say I have no right to invade her privacy, we've always given each other permission to access each other's phones and social media accounts at any time. Neither of us has anything to hide," he said pointedly.

"No, that's good. I'm glad you did it," Lani said. "Did you check private messages?"

He nodded. "Nothing interesting to note."

"Does Kira have any sneakers like these?" Jonah asked, holding the muddy shoe up.

Michael looked at them and shrugged. "I have no idea. We don't work out together. Maybe, I guess."

"We'll send it over to the MPD for evidence. Just in case," the SAR leader said, then he and his partner walked away.

"What did you tell the boys about Kira?" Lani asked Michael.

"I told them she was taking a few days to go to a Mommy-retreat."

"And they bought that?" Jonah asked.

"I think so, but Micah said he was mad at her for not saying goodbye."

"How are you holding up?" Lani asked.

"I didn't sleep last night. I know Kira's out there and she's probably cold and afraid." He looked down at the ground.

At least he was worried from a warm, comfortable bed. Not a too-short pickup cab with mosquitos torturing him with their incessant buzzing around his ears. Jonah reminded himself that he had personally encouraged Michael to go home and stay with the boys, to try to keep things as normal as possible for them.

"Don't think about that," Lani said to Michael. "You'll put negative vibes out into the universe. We need to visualize her strong. Capable."

"I'll visualize her walking out of there and that's about as positive as I can get," Jonah said.

"They took my car for processing," Michael said. "I'm going to need a ride to get the kids later."

"They want mine too. So ridiculous," Jonah said.

"You're telling me," Michael replied. "Of course, they're going to find evidence of Kira all over my car.

She's my wife—not some stranger who shouldn't be in my car."

"I think they're just trying to put pressure on you," Lani said.

"Pressure for what? I've done nothing wrong. I was on a damn boat when she disappeared! I've already given them the names of everyone on that charter. Also, plenty of my buddies saw me at the dock before and after. All they need to do is make a few calls to verify my story and stop wasting precious time investigating me."

"Well, technically, you can't prove you were on the boat when she disappeared. It's only confirmed you were there at your regular shift, but they don't know what time Kira actually went missing. It could've been before you left the dock."

Michael glared at Lani.

"So far, they're saying they don't have a person of interest, but I'm not so sure they aren't taking both of you seriously," Lani continued, her gaze going from Michael to Jonah. "Not to alarm you guys."

"I'm not alarmed. They can look at me all the want. They're not going to get anywhere, though," Jonah said.

"Of course they're looking at me. The husband is always the first person of interest," Michael said. "I just wish they'd clear me so they could focus on other leads."

"If we had any," Lani said.

Jonah looked up to see Kim coming at him.

She greeted him and came in for a hug.

He couldn't deny that having her in his arms brought him a sudden rush of comfort. He held on tight.

"We'll leave you two alone to talk a minute," Lani said, nudging Michael to go with her.

"Hi," Jonah murmured into her hair. He inhaled deeply, appreciating the scent of her shampoo. She always smelled delicious. "I thought you were going back to the hospital when you woke up from your nap?"

"I am. But I wanted to see you first. Make sure you're okay." She stepped back and dug through the big bag she had looped over her shoulder.

"What's that?"

"Fortification," she said, then handed him a bottle of orange juice and a muffin. "You're going through a lot of electrolytes out here. I know there's probably donated stuff for you to eat, but I'm going to watch and make sure you have this before I go."

"I'm fine," Jonah said, but inside it felt good to have someone care about him. Especially after such a lonely night.

"I'll decide that. Eat up. Drink the juice." She stood back and crossed her arms. "Has anyone found anything out there?"

He took a bite of the muffin and shook his head. "A shoe. But we don't think it's hers. What do you think they'll do next for Mom?"

Kim tilted her head, thinking for a second. "They can't do a lot, Jonah. They'll monitor her and possibly even do a scan to see how much blood has drained from her brain. They'll keep her warm and comfortable. It's basically a wait-and-see game right now."

"For how long?"

"We don't know. It's different for every stroke patient. I can tell you this, though. She's very lucky because the majority who have endured this type of injury die within a few hours. That she held on through the worst of it means a lot. Now the brain must rest to recover, so her being out is a good thing, even though it's scary."

Jonah wished he'd stopped eating. The crumbs were suddenly one big dry lump in his throat as he tried to swallow.

He kept his eyes downcast.

"Aww, babe," Kim said, then moved in and put her arms around him again. "I know this is a lot, but I promise your mom has a good medical team up there, and they're doing everything they can. You focus on Kira."

He nodded, then took a swig of the juice. Finally, the muffin went down. But he didn't look at Kim. If he did, and she saw the anguish in his eyes, he might lose it.

"I'm going to go over and talk to Maggie and Lani," Kim said. "Give you a minute. I'm sure they want an update too."

He turned away, grateful for her intuition. She was right. He needed a minute.

Or a time travel machine to take him back to yesterday morning, when the most troublesome thing in his life was his little sister ragging him about his love life. If only his worries could be so few now, or ever again.

Chapter Fifteen

The only way that Jules could determine night from day was the amount of activity around her. She surmised it was night when everything slowed down, and her pokes and prods were not as frequent. Thankfully, it was usually then that she was able to slip in and out of slumber and tried to spend as much time there as she could, hoping it would allow her brain enough rest to wake up. She felt like an infant, but the heaviness of her body told her that wasn't so. Yet she couldn't talk. Couldn't walk. And was truly at the mercy of those around her.

She was cold.

But she couldn't tell them.

Her back ached.

Another silent burden.

She could hear.

But she couldn't respond—not even when it came to her own care.

Noah's voice broke through. "Kim, when she wakes up, what do you think we are looking at as far as rehabilitation?"

"It's hard to say. The hemorrhage happened on the left side of her brain, which controls language and logic, but we've come a long way in stroke research to know that the brain has the power to heal itself if there's still enough living cells to begin the rebuilding process."

"How does that work? Therapy?"

"There's conflicting advice about what works best, but what we do know is that the part of the brain that is damaged has to be nurtured and sometimes taught to retrieve information in a new, different way than it did before the stroke."

It felt like night now and while they talked around her, Jules let her thoughts wander to what it would be like if that invisible tether broke and she was able to visit the state of euphoria again, but this time on a permanent basis. She wondered if there was more to it—and if the place she entered was only the prelude, like a front porch to the paradise she'd always thought she'd go to upon her death.

There was more movement around her. More talking. Most of it indistinguishable to Jules as it was said too quickly, not giving her a chance to work through the sounds and link them to any meaning.

It was exhausting even trying.

"Dad, Helen, I'd like some time alone with Mom if you don't mind."

"Of course."

Jules heard more noise, then silence. She felt a sudden layer of weight, and a welcome warmth spread over her.

"Here's a warm blanket, Mom. I think you can hear me. It's Quinn. I have something that needs to be said and I don't want it to wait another minute."

A lapse, then more words.

"I know that you've had to carry a lot of guilt and worry because of what happened to me so long ago, but I want to thank you for accepting me back into the family. You could've closed that door, knowing it would bring back bad memories while inviting a perfect stranger into your lives, but you've taught me how to embrace people and experiences with an open heart."

The voice soothed Jules. At first, she thought she didn't recognize it, but as it continued, a familiar feeling came over her.

Quinn. *Her* Quinn. Who had once been lost. The memory reminded her that Kira was lost now, and she couldn't do anything about it. The feeling of helplessness was so huge that it made her body feel weaker. As Quinn talked on, Jules allowed herself to sink back into her dream world, where she wouldn't have to face the very real possibility of losing another daughter.

Day Three

Chapter Sixteen

This was it. If the SAR team didn't find Kira by sundown, they'd be on their own. Jonah stood deathly still, Derek at his side and Detective Kamaka in front, blocking his view to the forest.

Jonah fumed. He could barely believe that island resources only allowed seventy-two hours for a missing person search. The forest was nearly endless, so dense with too many gulches. It couldn't possibly be searched thoroughly in that short amount of time.

No wonder Maui had at least two dozen names still on its missing persons list. People disappeared and after only a few days of a ground search, their families were then expected to provide the resources to find them, which for many wasn't an option. Not every family had a Helen Rocha in its arsenal, and even if it did, that didn't guarantee that they would be able to find Kira.

A commotion sounded behind him and Jonah turned to see Michael breaking away from Lani, who was trying to hold him back.

"A damn shame," Michael ranted, stomping over until he stood eye-to-eye with the detective.

"What's going on?" Jonah demanded. He pulled on Michael's arm, trying to put more space between him and a rattled Kamaka.

"He knows what the hell is going on. Ask him!" Michael jabbed his finger into the detective's chest and this time, Jonah used all the strength he had to yank him a few feet back.

Derek grabbed Michael's other arm and together they kept him from lunging forward.

"You'd better check yourself," the detective said. "I could have you sitting in a jail cell, praying someone tells you what the hell is happening in your wife's case."

"That's exactly what I'm doing now; I might as well be in a jail cell," Michael shouted. "You won't tell me a damn thing, and now you're putting rumors out there to make me look guilty."

"Slow down and tell me what you're talking about," Jonah said, looking from the detective and back to Michael.

"According to all the news outlets this morning," Michael said, "My trip for garden supplies at the Home Depot last week makes me a likely suspect."

"What are you talking about?" Jonah asked.

"Didn't Kira tell you about the garden we started? I bought a new shovel and rake, and some lime for conditioning. Someone pulled the footage of me at the register and it's all over the place now."

Jonah felt his stomach drop, and he saw Derek grimace. It was only six in the morning and already the day was going to hell in a handbasket.

"Did your sister speak of a garden to you?" the detective asked Jonah.

He wracked his brain, trying to remember.

"Oh, yes, she did. She said they were doing it to teach the boys how to be less wasteful with food. And you're using that as evidence?" Jonah asked, bewildered.

"I'm not at liberty to talk about any evidence we have or haven't located, but I can tell you that there have not been any official announcements made by the department."

Michael tried to thrust free, but Jonah held him.

"It's bullshit, Jonah," Michael said. "A tactic to put pressure on me. You either did it or you've got a mole at the department, Kamaka. Someone who likes to post false news all over the internet to make innocent people out to be criminals."

Kamaka looked guilty. Jonah was immediately suspicious.

Lani joined them. "Stop this. This is the last thing our volunteers need to hear about. Get a hold of yourself, Michael. I saw the footage too, and you don't see me throwing a tantrum or accusing you of burying your wife."

"I completely agree," Kamaka said. "You're making quite the spectacle over a little thing. If this is your best attempt at an 'innocent husband act,' I don't see any cameras, so it's wasted on just me."

Jonah had to hang on tighter. He could feel Michael trembling with rage.

"I'm going to sue every last one of you if it's the last thing I do," Michael sputtered.

Lani shook her head. "Don't get all righteous on us, Detective Kamaka. Maybe it wasn't you, but someone in your department planted that rumor and we don't need anyone turning against us right now. We need to bring Kira back home, and that should be your primary focus too. That's what our grandmother is sponsoring you to do, if you need a reminder."

The detective raised his eyebrows. "I'll treat this case just like I would for any family, regardless of their monetary worth."

"Then stop focusing on me and help me find my wife," Michael exclaimed. "And let us do our part here to see if she's in there."

"I'll try to find out who leaked the footage," the detective said, finally conceding. "It's done now, and I apologize on behalf of the department if someone there leaked it. I can do that much. What I *can't* do is take you off the table completely as a person of interest in this case. To put it mildly, you aren't doing yourself any favors, so I'd advise calming down for starters."

Jonah could feel the tension in Michael starting to simmer down and he let him go. "What else do we need to anticipate coming to the surface that might make Michael look guilty?"

"What about a life insurance policy?" the detective asked. "Do you have one on your wife?"

They all looked at Michael.

He shook loose of Jonah and Derek, then straightened his shirt and stood tall.

"Yes, we have life insurance policies. Don't most couples who run a business together?"

Derek's phone buzzed and he left the group to answer it.

"Is it for more than what's covered under the company umbrella?" Lani asked quietly.

Michael looked hurt at her question, but he answered.

"Yes. It was Kira's idea. She said if one of us dies, the other will need enough money to replace that salary, as well as pay for more childcare. We have the same amount on me, too."

He looked from Jonah to Lani, his tone pleading now. "We thought it was the responsible thing to do."

Jonah didn't know what to think now. Only the year before, his sister and Michael had been pinching every penny in order to one day buy their own business. Now they were paying for extra life insurance premiums.

Things were getting complicated.

He pushed the dark thoughts away. Right now, he wanted to concentrate on finding Kira and not let his mind—or public opinion—talk him into something more sinister.

She was out there.

And they had to find her today.

"What are you going to do next to find my wife? Other than painting me as guilty. That's the real question," Michael demanded.

"I'll need to question Quinn and Lani again. I also need a list of Kira's friends and colleagues she comes in contact with on a daily basis. We did put out an official plea to the public yesterday evening on the news, in case you haven't seen it," he said.

"Yeah, I saw it." Michael said.

"Me too," Lani echoed.

"I haven't." Jonah said. "A plea stating what, exactly?"

"We showed photos of Kira and of her car. We asked for the public's help providing information of her whereabouts and told them to contact us at the MPD."

Jonah's temper flared and he pointed at the jungle. "We *know* her whereabouts. She's in there!"

"That has not been proven thus far. The search teams haven't found any evidence to show she ever stepped foot on the trail," the detective said. "And not to throw this on you in a bad moment, Mr. Monroe, but we still need to take your truck for processing."

"They already went through it yesterday."

He had allowed the detectives access to his vehicle the day before and they'd gone over it with a fine-toothed comb. It had gutted him. A man's truck was like an extension of himself and having it pawed over just felt dirty.

"We need to take it to the lab for a more thorough look."

"Fine. You want the piece of shit, take it," Jonah said, then reached into his pocket and pulled out his keys and threw them at the man. Without quick reflexes, the keys probably would've put out an eye. But Jonah couldn't care less. "And yes, Kira has been in my truck before. Do you seriously think I have something to do with my sister's disappearance? What kind of sicko do you think I am?"

"Not saying that, Mr. Monroe. But we have to eliminate those closest to her. That's how an investigation works."

Jonah nearly said another smartass remark, but Derek happened to return at that moment. He reached over and put a hand on Jonah's shoulder. His friend knew him well enough to realize he was about to lose it. Jonah never showed disrespect to someone in authority, but he was at the end of his rope.

"We haven't given up yet, man," Derek reassured him. "We are still trying to get someone to donate their helicopter and the fuel. I've also got two drones going up in an hour."

Jonah nodded. He appreciated that his friend was pulling in every favor he could. This was a volunteer position for him, and he hadn't worked at his real job since he'd shown up at the reserve the first day. He was a good guy. The best. Still, things weren't looking good. But if Jonah had learned anything in the service, it was to keep moving forward toward the objective. Standing still made you a sitting duck and going backward was never an option. It was just getting harder every minute that she wasn't found.

"Don't get down, Jonah," Derek said. "I need you to be positive. Manifest what you want to happen. *See her.* Then we'll find her."

"I'm okay." But he wasn't. He'd slept in his truck

again and was wearing the same jeans he'd worn since the morning he'd met Kira for their late breakfast. He'd run home and gotten a clean shirt and socks, at least, but had only stayed long enough to check on things before coming straight back to the reserve.

Even being gone for that short amount of time had made him feel guilty for leaving Kira. He'd climbed out of the truck and screamed her name, letting her know he was back. Then it was another long night trying to find a comfortable position for his long, lanky body.

His phone rang and he saw Kim's face flash on his screen. He turned away to take the call and walked in the other direction.

"Jonah, hi." Kim's tone was in no-nonsense work mode, but it carried a hint of something else in it…sympathy, which terrified him.

"Hey, babe. What's going on up there?"

He heard Kim let out a big sigh. "This is hard to say. The doc on duty talked to your dad about signing a DNR."

"What is that?"

"It's a do not resuscitate order."

Jonah felt nauseous. "What the hell? It's only been a few days!"

He felt Lani come up behind him and lean in. He switched to speaker, so she could hear.

"Your dad said no. And I talked to him and Quinn after the doctor left. It's not uncommon for these doctors to push people into signing them, but I think he should wait and see what happens with your mom over the next few days. Unfortunately, the hospital admin wants these patients off care that require a trained nurse present at all times. They are always short on staff and that contributes to the early push. When it comes down to it, it's all about what her care is costing the hospital."

Jonah breathed deeply, trying to control the anger in his voice before he spoke.

"I'm glad you were there, Kim. I can't thank you enough. I know Dad—all of us—feel better knowing that you're there, advocating for us, and that you believe in Mom."

"You don't have to thank me. This is what family does. We're there for each other."

Uncomfortable pause.

Because Jonah didn't know what to say. There was no doubt that he cared about Kim deeply, but he wasn't so sure about making it official. She didn't know how screwed up he was and how hard it could be to be a member of his family.

"The doctor also told them that she won't regain the parts of her brain that were damaged," Kim said, filling in the awkward silence. "In my opinion, he has no basis for saying that. Not yet anyway. There's just as good of a chance that things will get better as there is that they will get worse. It is way too early to write her off. I've been studying neuroplasticity as an area of expertise, and studies show that it's possible for her brain to make a complete recovery. But she needs time."

"She needs a new doctor," he said.

"He's just one part of a team. The next one might say something different, but they all face pressure from the upper levels."

Jonah let out a long sigh. He'd give anything to be there with his mom, but he had to focus on Kira.

For Mom.

"I need to go, Kim. I'm trying to keep tabs on the SAR teams, and they're briefing now." He didn't burden her with the current situation involving the detective and Michael sparring back and forth.

"Wait. Have you eaten this morning, Jonah?"

"Yes, I had some fruit," he lied. The truth was that he couldn't eat a bite. But he'd had plenty of coffee to keep him going. "Talk to you later."

He'd barely hung up when Maggie joined them, her face a mask of anger.

"We've got trolls all over our *Find Kira* page. Someone went in last night and posted that you're all rich, entitled land thieves and it serves you right to lose her."

Lani nodded. "I saw that, too. And they're telling the public not to help in any way. The tide is turning against us fast."

"Damn. That's going to hurt. SAR is pulling out after today and we necd some experienced hikers to keep up the search. I was depending on some volunteers to come forward."

"I just saw the newest comments ten minutes ago," Maggie said. "People are getting ugly."

Jonah felt a hell of a headache coming his way. While the old story was true, and his great-grandfather did steal the land from the Crowes so many years ago, he also knew that his grandmother had eventually made it right. Not only had she signed parcels of land over to members of the Crowe family for no more than a dollar an acre, but she'd also set up scholarships for half a dozen of the heirs.

That wasn't the first steps she'd made as restitution either. Since his grandfather had died, his grandmother had voluntarily given many gifts to the city of Maui and was one of the first citizens they called on when in a financial pinch.

"Carmen needs to come forward somehow," Lani said. "She is the only one who can erase the stain from our family's reputation and get the people on our side. We can't do this alone. We need help."

Jonah agreed, but Carmen, his grandmother's friend

and a member of the Crowe family, was somewhat of a recluse. She had been involved in Quinn's abduction so many years ago. She'd done what she could to make amends, but since then she'd barely come out into the public arena, choosing to do her philanthropic endeavors from the safety of her own home.

"She probably won't want to get involved in yet another media firestorm, especially one that deals with the disappearance of a Rocha heir," he said

Jonah heard a commotion and saw Derek grab a black bag and run toward the trailhead, barking orders into his cellphone. Members of his team followed and one of them carried a cot.

He felt his pulse suddenly race and his heartbeat pound in his ears.

"They must've found her," he said, then took off running, his sister and Maggie right on his heels.

Chapter Seventeen

Jules looked at her watch and then at the gloomy sky. Noah was late bringing the clients up. She stared at the black cloud that had appeared and parked itself directly over them. The wind stirred as well, and Jules could feel the storm coming. It was going to be a mad dash to the harbor and if the clients got drenched, Noah could kiss their tip goodbye.

"Mom, where are they?" Jonah asked, his young face crinkled with worry.

He hated to be on the water when it stormed.

"They should be coming up in a minute," she replied.

Nama glanced up at her. Her deep brown eyes searching.

"It's fine, sweetie. Daddy's on his way," Jules reassured her.

Nama nodded and turned her attention back to her dolls. She wasn't afraid of storms—not like Jonah. Then again, Jonah worried about everything.

Jules went to a seat and pulled it up, grabbing two raincoats from within. She handed one to Jonah, who immediately pulled it on, then she went to Nama.

"I don't want to wear it," Nama said, shaking her off when Jules tried to guide it around her shoulders.

Suddenly a crack of lightning hit the water only a few

yards from the boat and thunder rumbled.

"Mom," Jonah said, his voice trailing out in a question of uncertainty.

"You both get under here," Jules said, guiding them under the small awning. They'd have to share it with the clients on the way back in, but it was inevitable, the kids were about to get wet. And the clients were going to feel the drops on their backs, too.

Jules always found it strange that their clients didn't mind getting wet in the ocean, but they abhorred getting rained on while in the boat.

She looked at her watch again and silently cursed. Where were they? Couldn't Noah see the storm brewing toward the surface?

A decision needed to be made.

Either go get them and possibly outrun the storm, or worst-case scenario, wait for them like a sitting duck and deal with the clients' moans and groans as they got drenched on the way back in. Also, with the lightning so close, it was a dangerous liability.

They needed to get a move on. And fast.

"Jonah, I'm going to have to go down and wave to your dad," she said. "He needs to get the clients up here stat."

Her son looked fearful and that sent a dagger to her heart.

"Be a big boy and look after your sister," she said as she quickly finished suiting up. She didn't feel good about her decision.

Not at all.

Was that her gut telling her to wait? Or just warning her to hurry?

The sky got even darker as she hesitated.

"Just go, Mom," Jonah said, seeming to read her mind.

"Okay, but you get Nama into her raincoat while I'm gone. I'll be back in a flash, I promise."

Quickly she kissed them both on the top of their heads, reminded Jonah to look after Nama, adjusted her face mask, then flipped backwards over the side of the boat.

Despite her anxiety, Jules embraced the peaceful feeling of the deep water, cutting through as graceful as a fish as the blissful silence immediately engulfed her. She adored the sensation of slow-motion freedom as she looked deeper, searching into the blue.

Jules tried to move her hand, then remembered she was still stuck, a prisoner in her own useless body. She could feel her heart pounding almost as much as she could still smell the sea and view the darkness of the water.

It was gone now.

But it had felt so real.

And so had the feeling of dread that began to swallow her up as soon as she'd hit the water. A warning of sorts. But of what?

She heard a sudden series of beeps and a commotion around her.

"What's going on?" Quinn said.

"It's her blood pressure again. Something has upset her." A brisk voice. All business. "Back away from the bed."

"Fine. But I wasn't even talking anymore. I was just holding her hand quietly."

A door opened, then Jules heard Noah.

"Quinn? Is everything okay?"

"Mom's struggling."

Jules felt Noah come close and she longed to reach for

him, knowing his touch would bring her fears to a halt.

He put his hand over hers. "I'm here, Jules."

A sense of peace surrounded her, blocking out the heavy fear. The dread of something she couldn't remember.

"It's coming down," a voice said. "She's back in normal range. I think we should limit her visitors for the rest of the day."

"I'm not leaving her," Noah said. "I'll sit in the hall outside the door if I have to, but I'm not going anywhere."

The brisk voice again. "All of you need to prepare yourselves for the possibility that she might not wake up. The longer a patient is in a coma, the less of a chance at survival they have."

"Please don't talk like that in front of my wife," Noah said.

Jules could feel his anger.

"I'm only trying to be the voice of reason. And she can't hear me. I'll get the doctor to sign off on only one visitor at a time for today."

A small silence.

"I'll go," said Quinn, finally. "Dad, you stay. It's clear that you make her calm just by being here. Something is going on with her today. I can feel it. You need to be with her."

"Well, then, I hope we can keep Helen at bay," Noah answered. "But she's determined to come back tomorrow for some time alone with your mom."

"I know," said Quinn. "She's hurting too. Her fears are getting the best of her. Between mom being in here and, well… you know, the other situation. I can only imagine that she's afraid things will be forever left unsaid."

"That's not going to happen. There will be plenty of time to say things when your mom recovers. Go on and get some rest today, Quinn. We'll be fine."

Jules heard the door shut and then felt Noah's warm lips on her forehead. Even without sight, there was no mistaking them.

"Oh, my Jules of the Sea. I miss you. And I need you to come back to us."

Jules willed her eyes to open. He was so close. She could feel his breath on her cheek. The agony in his voice made her sad to the depths of her soul.

"Quinn will be back later," he said.

He paused and Jules thought he might've left the room before he began again, in a softer tone. "We got us a good one, Jules. All those years we missed our little girl. Who would've thought she would grow into such a kind, strong woman? She's just like you, you know. Would do anything to help everyone in her path."

Jules listened and this time was able to catch every word. Noah—her Noah—he spoke softly and calmly. Like he knew he needed to speak slowly for her to understand.

She heard sudden pain in his voice.

"I don't think I'll ever stop wondering about who she was at age five. And ten. Then as a teenage girl. She went through everything without us, Jules. Our little Nama. Our tiny sea nymph. It wouldn't be right if you were deprived of any more time with her, with us, finally as a full family again. Please come back to us, Jules."

She felt a tear drop from his cheek onto her hand and it brought her back to the sea, going down, down.

She found Noah and the guests gathered around a few large rocks and saw a manta ray slide out from under and skim across the bottom.

As soon as Noah saw her, he looked surprised, then alarmed.

He held up his hands as though to ask what was going on.

She gave him the gesture to come up right away, then gave a kick and headed for the surface. It hadn't been more than ten minutes since she'd been down but as she got closer to the boat, the water was visibly choppier, and she could see the bottom of the vessel rocking back and forth.

With a last upward surge, she broke the water and hunched forward against the pounding rain. Before she could recover from the onslaught, she was blown back, and she struggled to make headway.

The storm had developed into much more than a minor squall. The bottom had fallen out of the sky and the wind had increased by multiple notches. By now, the waves were cresting higher and higher and she dreaded the trip back to the dock.

Jules swam hard, aiming for the boat. At this point, she no longer cared about the tip. She just wanted to get everyone to the dock safely.

And she especially wanted to get back to her kids.

Finally, she reached the ladder and climbed up and into the boat. She looked for Jonah, sure he'd be watching for her.

But there was no one there.

She pulled off her mask, certain her eyes were playing tricks on her, but when she blinked and looked again, nothing had changed.

Other than most of the unsecured contents strewn into one corner, including a few life vests and a snack bag, the boat was empty.

Jules felt a cold snake of fear shimmy down her spine.

Her children were gone.

Chapter Eighteen

Helen sat at her kitchen table with her arsenal in front of her. Laptop, notebook, pen, and phone. And a pot of coffee brewing.

Her second pot of the day.

Next to her, she'd created a cradle of sorts for Cinder. She pulled two kitchen chairs together then put the little faux fur dog bed in it.

Cinder loved that she could burrow down into it and now only her nose and little dark eyes peeked out over the side. She was as close to Helen as she could get without being on her lap. That wasn't an option this morning because Helen had work to do. If she couldn't talk her daughter out of her coma, then the least she could do was work to bring Kira home. If she could do that, maybe she could bring Jules back too.

She glanced at her phone again. Silent. No blinking light to alert her of missed messages or calls. No one cared to keep her in the loop with any updates. She pledged to herself she wouldn't call anyone yet. She wouldn't beg for information.

At least not for another hour. Maybe by then someone would contact her.

A knock at the door startled her.

She looked up to see the silhouette of George through

the window.

"Come in," she called out.

He came through the door, his familiar smile calming her.

"Morning," she said, then looked back down.

He nodded and went to the counter, poured himself a cup of coffee, then cut off a small piece of banana bread and brought both to the table. He gave Cinder a pat before he pulled out a chair and sat down.

He looked at the picture of Jules and Nama that still lay on the table, but he didn't say anything about it.

"It's going to rain this afternoon," he finally said, his voice a low, gravely rumble.

"Good," Helen replied. "The garden will appreciate it."

"Anything you want to talk about?" he asked.

"Did you clean up around the hibiscus?"

"Sure did. I cleaned up some of the stone dust too. A few places in the wall are coming loose. Might need to get someone who knows what they are doing to come do some repairs."

"Okay, I'll take a look later." Helen jotted a note about it to remind herself.

"Anything else you want to talk about? Other than the garden?"

Helen sighed and put her pen down. He always seemed to know when something heavy was on her mind.

She looked at him.

There was a crumb sticking to his cheek and she nearly reached over and brushed it away before she stopped herself.

"Oh, George. Once again, my life is a mess."

He barely reacted. "Perhaps you need another perspective. Might do you good to talk about it."

Helen appreciated his ways. His voice low and quiet,

not prying, only inviting. If she told him she didn't want to talk, he'd be just fine with a quiet coffee time, then off to work outside he'd go. Over the last decade, he'd been the only one she'd really complained to about anything. She knew with George her words would go no further than her kitchen. And for a gardener—maybe even because he was a gardener—he had a lot of wisdom and good advice.

"Kira is missing," she said.

He nodded. "I heard that. I'm so sorry."

She raised her eyebrows. "You already knew?"

"I did. The whole town is buzzing about it."

"Supposedly she's lost in the Makawao Reserve," Helen said. "But I just don't know. There's no evidence that she even went in there. To be honest, I've never really trusted that husband of hers. He's not a local. Makes me suspicious."

"I wasn't a local either. And so far, I've kept a fairly clean nose," George said.

"Well, you're different."

He chuckled. "So, I know that brain of yours is spinning. What are you planning to do? Other than waterboarding Michael if you can get ahold of him."

"I'm not sure what I *can* do," Helen said, frowning over her notepad. "There are teams searching the forest, but they are only granted seventy-two hours of time, and that's about up.

Jonah and Lani are there watching over everything. Jonah is convinced there isn't any foul play involved and is putting all his concentration into the search. No one is pushing the actual investigation side of it, as far as I can tell. My efforts to contact the mayor were a bust, so I called the chief of police this morning."

"And?"

She tapped her pen against the wooden table. "He

wouldn't tell me anything."

"That's because he can't. He could lose his job for that, Helen. It's an open investigation. You know how that goes," he said, his voice gently scolding.

Oh, how she knew. Helen remembered so long ago in the first days after Nama went missing. None of the strings they tried to pull could get them insider information.

"The chief lectured me about the many people who go missing on Maui because they want to disappear. To escape their problems," she said.

"Kira would never do that." George scowled.

He was right about that. Kira might have a spirited soul, but she would never take off and leave her family to suffer and her children to grow up without a mother.

"I agree."

George knew Kira well too. He'd taught her a lot about different plants and flowers over the years when she'd come to visit and had found herself gravitating toward the garden. Helen liked to think that Kira had inherited her green thumb, though with her being a young wife and mother, she was much too busy to ever cultivate it with her own garden.

"If she's out there, she can survive as long as she finds water. And she knows how to do that," he said.

"There is that." Helen tried to remain hopeful, despite the rock in the pit of her stomach.

"She also knows many plants and berries that are edible. I taught her myself." He finished off the bread and stood.

Helen was grateful for that reminder. It was something she could cling to.

"I asked the chief about giving Michael a lie detector test and he ended the phone call." She was still steamed. No one hung up on her. Ever.

"Is there anything I can do to help?" He bent down in front of Cinder and tickled her behind her ears. Cinder's tail wiggled in delight.

She was a good judge of character.

"Not that I can think of, George. But I'll let you know if anything comes up."

"I'm going to get to work then. I'll be outside if you need me."

"I'll have you a sandwich ready at noon."

"Much appreciated," he said, ducking out the door and letting it close softly behind him.

She didn't have to feed him, but it made her life less lonely to have another human being stop in and out of her kitchen a few times a week. George never went into any other part of the house unless she needed some sort of assistance with a light bulb or an air filter—something like that. Then there was that time the plumbing backed up into her bathtub and she was so horrified by the mess that he sent her on a long drive while he and a gallon of bleach went to work cleaning it up. She'd been embarrassed that he'd seen her array of makeup and creams, everything she threw at her face to try to hide eighty years of hardships.

After George left, she called around until she got the name of the man in charge of the Maui Search and Rescue. But that call had gone nowhere too. She tried Jonah's phone again, but it went to voicemail. They had obviously forgotten that she was waiting for news—any at all.

The photograph of Jules with Nama was in front of her on the table.

Helen picked it up and stared at it, sighing long and loud.

Nama was such a beautiful girl. She'd looked exactly like Jules, but in miniature. Helen could still recall every

tiny detail from the day Quinn had been swept off that
boat and Jules had called her, begging her to do something, anything, to help.

Helen wished she could turn back time and go back to
the day so long ago when Carmen had called her to say
she had Nama in her care—that she'd found her washed
up at the beach. If only Helen had reacted differently
and not allowed her fear and paranoia to set in. Superstition ran deep in her family, and it had caused her to
make such a mistake. One that she knew could never
really be forgiven. Or at least hadn't been so far. And if
her Jules didn't return to them, Helen would have to live
until her dying day with the fact that she would never
be forgiven.

Cinder stood up in her bed, putting her paws on the
edge of the table as she barked, snapping Helen out of
her dark mire of memories.

"Be careful or you'll fall out of that chair. Just what do
you want, Miss Sassy-Pants?" she asked the dog. "Is it
time for your lunch?"

Then she smiled, thinking what her father would have
said about a dog sitting at the table. Helen was glad the
mean old bastard was dead if she was being totally honest with herself.

She looked at her phone.

Who could she call? Who could possibly put her family back together again?

She didn't know.

The picture caught her eye again, reminding her that
they'd already been through this once. Maybe the curse
meant that she would have to live through the horror all
over again, but this time with a double punch of losing
two people she loved, instead of just one.

"Cinder, girl, after I make George a sandwich I'm
going to need to go back to the hospital. Think you can

hold the fort down again?"

The dog looked up at her, her little snout scrunched up in a disappointed expression. Like she was judging.

Or perhaps she always looked like that. Helen wasn't sure. All she was sure about was that she needed to get herself together and do something before she lost everything that mattered to her.

Day Four

Chapter Nineteen

The false alarm from the day before had Jonah feeling discouraged. What he and Lani had hoped was a cot going in to pull Kira out of the reserve was actually intended for one of the rescuers. A young guy on the first team had gotten a little too eager and decided to climb an old tree without checking with someone more experienced. He was already inching out on a dead branch before someone could warn him, and he'd hit the ground from about twenty feet high.

The guy was lucky. He'd be fine other than a mild concussion and a broken collarbone, but he'd probably never want to climb another tree again.

The rest of the day and evening had led to nothing. Jonah had fallen into his tent completely depleted, emotionally and physically, and dreading the moment his dad would call to check in.

He followed Derek out of the jungle, his heart in his throat.

Jonah could thank the bond of friendships for squeezing one more day out of the Maui search and rescue team. However, despite canvasing every square inch of their grid, they still hadn't found Kira nor a scrap of evidence that she'd been there. He wanted to push out of the expected edges to search other areas but was told repeatedly that if Kira were in the reserve, she could only be within the boundaries the search team had predicted.

But what if they were wrong?

He wanted to yell at the universe—maybe cuss it a little—but someone had to be the strong and steady one. He was the sibling in charge—the older brother—a factor he was reminded of immediately as he approached the parking lot and saw Lani and Maggie. Quinn too.

He was nearly too ashamed to look at them but realized if Quinn had left their mother's side, she must have come to deliver bad news.

"What's going on?"

"Don't freak out. Mom's status hasn't changed. But we need you to go with us somewhere," Quinn said.

"Where?"

"You'll see. We're going to make sure this search continues one way or another. "We're not giving up. We're just trying a different avenue."

"I don't understand, and I also don't have time for field trips," Jonah replied.

Whether the search team was going back in or not, he knew he would be in there again as soon as he rested for a few minutes.

"We can't let this lead get away from us," Lani said.

"Explain." He looked around, found an oversized rock, and took a seat.

The girls followed, standing around him in a protective half-circle.

"You remember Maria, the woman who owned the house I bought in Kihei when I first arrived on Maui? We're going to see her Kupuna." Quinn said. "He's our best chance for changing the tide of community outrage against our family."

"And we need this community more than ever," Lani

added.

Jonah ran his hands through his hair. In their culture, going to the elders in the midst of a crisis was a common ritual. They provided guidance and wisdom that their older years had earned them. Even going to seek guidance would earn them some points with their town.

But he didn't want to leave Makawao. Or Kira.

He looked back at the jungle behind him.

There was still so much of it that hadn't been touched. And backup volunteers had dropped off dramatically, leaving them with nowhere near enough manpower to cover much past the grid the SAR team had created.

"Can't you go without me? I want to keep searching. It will be dark soon," he said finally. He respected every Kupuna, but he didn't have a lot of confidence that one man was powerful enough to sway so many in their favor.

"It would be better to be united as a family," Quinn said.

Michael joined them, his hair wet with sweat as he wiped his face with his bandana. Jonah wasn't sure what he'd been doing, but at least he was keeping busy.

"I agree. You need to go," he said. "I got things here."

"You talked to him before you talked to me?" Jonah asked Lani, feeling his temper flare.

Before Lani could even answer, Michael straightened up as though a puppet master had just pulled his string.

"Listen. I've held my tongue so far and let you take the lead because I know that what you went through all those years ago has been eating you alive, making this whole thing even harder on you. I know you're terrified to lose another sister. But dude, she's *my* wife. And you're making it harder on me than it should be."

"What the hell have I done to you?" Jonah couldn't believe what he was hearing.

"You keep pushing me away, man. It makes me look guilty to everyone else that I'm not leading the charge. Like I don't care," Michael said, his voice breaking. "I care. That's my wife and my baby out there."

Jonah froze. Had he heard what he thought he heard?

"Your baby?" Lani asked, jumping on it immediately.

Michael dropped to a squat and covered his face. He rocked back and forth.

"Yes, my baby. Kira is pregnant, alright? We weren't going to tell anyone about it until she was a little further along. And we wanted to have a game plan in place about how to handle childcare with another one in the mix. That's what we argued about the day that Kira went missing. She said she wanted to stay home with this baby. Be there for the boys after school, too, but I told her we couldn't afford it."

The words were muffled through his fingers, but clear enough to pick up.

"God—I wish I could have that conversation over again," Michael said. "I'm such an idiot. So damn stupid."

Jonah felt sick to his stomach.

This revelation changed everything.

"Stand up and talk to me like a man," Jonah said, ignoring the angry look from both Lani and Quinn that his words brought on.

Michael stood and lifted his chin proudly, his fists balled at his sides even as his face shone with tears.

"I need you to look me in the eye and tell me if you hurt Kira. This is it, Michael. No more games." He'd tried to be calm, but he knew his voice was steeled for conflict.

"Jonah," Lani scolded.

"I did *not* hurt Kira. I *would never* hurt Kira. Nor my child. Ever," Michael said, enunciating each word carefully and strongly.

They locked eyes, each waiting for the other to look away. Jonah searched for dishonesty. For anything that would indicate betrayal.

Michael stayed firm, his stance daring Jonah to doubt him.

"Quit posturing, you two. Let's focus. This cannot get out about the baby," Quinn said. "If the public gets wind of it, they'll come after Michael with a pitchfork. Keep this quiet, and we all need to think about what Kira would want right now. I guarantee she would tell you to work together. That we are all—*every one of us*—family."

"She's right, guys. Quit carrying your asses on your shoulders. I'm a good judge of deceit and I can tell you, Michael hasn't hurt Kira. She's still out there. We need to get back to our next steps," Maggie said. "We have to keep going, and believe me, you don't want me to be the one to set you straight."

Jonah glared at her, though he wasn't surprised at her statement. Maggie was as spicy as they came, red hair and all. Even her rock-solid boyfriend couldn't temper her fiery side. She was scary as hell.

He relaxed his shoulders and stepped back.

Michael did the same.

"Good. That's put to bed. Now. I feel very strongly about meeting with the Kupuna," Quinn said. "I also think that is something that Kira would approve of, considering how devoted she is to our heritage."

At that moment, Derek approached them.

"Look, Jonah. I talked to the team and they've got one last round in them for today. We'll go in and spread just a bit further out. But I'm going to be honest with you, man. Most of them have to go back to work and they won't be here tomorrow. We need some volunteers, and from what I've seen today, they've stopped showing up. Lani told me the plan and if this guy is a well-respected Kupuna, it might just help."

Jonah considered. He didn't know Maria and her family well, so he couldn't say whether her father was a true Kupuna, but if he was, the title itself held an unbelievable amount of respect and awe. He could possibly have enough reach to at least get them another dozen or so volunteers who had experience in hiking difficult areas or even rappelling. That's what they needed—some really tough and knowledgeable people to replace the ones on the SAR team who wouldn't be coming back.

"Fine. And Derek," Jonah said, looking at his brother-in-law, "Just so you know, Michael's in charge."

"Got it," Derek said.

Michael nodded at Jonah, a stoic gesture of gratitude.

"Come on. We need to hurry," Quinn said. "It's a long drive to Kihei and we want to be back here before dark."

"I'll keep you posted if we find anything," Michael said.

"I know the way so I'm driving," Quinn said. "Maggie, I want you to come, too. They'll be glad to see you again after so long."

"You can have shotgun," Lani said to Jonah, opening the back door of Quinn's truck. "Maggie and I have notes to go over."

When they were loaded in and buckled up, Quinn reached behind her seat and pulled out a paper bag, then handed it to him before she pulled out onto the main road.

"It's your lunch. Kim sent it," she said, smiling at him. "She made me promise I'd watch you eat it. I told her that it would be my pleasure."

"I bet you did," he said, grimacing as he pulled out a small pouch of dried seaweed, a banana, and a bottle of organic noni juice.

"She said it will help keep your body in balance," Quinn said. She raised her eyebrows at Jonah, challenging him.

He shook his head and stuffed it back down into the bag. "No."

Maggie had mercy on him and handed him a bottle of water from somewhere behind his seat. He uncapped it and swigged nearly half of it in one go. Then he ate the banana, immediately feeling less exhausted.

"While we're all together, let's go over some search points," Lani said from the back seat.

Jonah leaned back, closing his eyes as he listened.

"It's possible that we've been wasting time— that Kira was snatched before she even got to the trail," Maggie said.

"Which is why I wish that parking lot had cameras!" Lani said, exasperated. "It would save a lot of time and effort if we knew whether she was in the jungle or not. But in the meantime, I'm planning to go door-to-door to as many houses as possible on the way to the reserve to see if any of them have cameras pointed toward the street," Lani said.

"What will that tell?" Jonah asked.

"It will tell us whether Kira was driving her car. Or if she was alone. She could've picked someone up to give them a ride and something happened when they got to the reserve. We need to get on it immediately since some footage expires after a few days."

Jonah didn't like to even consider that possibility, but his sister was right, they needed to begin pursuing other possibilities of what may have happened to Kira.

"If someone saw something, they would've said something," Jonah replied. "Don't you think?"

"Maybe not," Maggie said. "Some people don't even

have internet up there. Many are unplugged from every-thing and might not know Kira is missing. It won't hurt to see if any homes have cameras pointed their way or at least toward the street so we could see if she really left."

"You know the police have probably already done all that," he said.

"Maybe. But we don't know," Maggie said. "I've called repeatedly. I can't get anything out of them."

"We won't, either. At least nothing official until the investigation is over," Lani said.

"I've got our own detective on his way," Quinn said.

"What do you mean?" Jonah asked.

"Remember David and Julianne Westbrooks, our first guests at the inn? I called David and he is working with us, giving us directions to follow. Lani has already sent him a lot of the leads she's working on, but he's also going to make some calls."

Jonah did remember them and felt a moment of sad-ness. They were one of the most dedicated couples he had ever met. Julianne had passed away from cancer just a few weeks after they'd left Maui. Jonah had won-dered a few times how the man was getting by without her. Using his work as a distraction, he guessed.

"That's great," Jonah said. "I hope MPD won't shut him down."

"They can't," said Lani. "We're allowed to hire our own investigator as long as they don't interfere with the official investigation. They don't have to know he's doing it pro bono."

"We can use all the help we can get," said Maggie. "I'm trying to focus on organizing incoming tips. Lani is following up on the ones that sound viable as well as her own ideas."

He had to admit, Lani was doing a great job. When he'd checked on her earlier in the day, she was jotting down a list of names of anyone on the island who had been paroled in the weeks and days before Kira went missing. She was cross-referencing them with their crimes and noting those that were violent or charged with sexual abuse.

It seemed his sister had a knack for investigation. She also didn't let anyone give her any lip, which was a lethal combination.

They talked about the reporter, Simon Lang, and how he'd hung back from snooping around. What they didn't know was that Jonah had threatened him with a restraining order, so the man was keeping just far enough out of their hair to take note of what was happening without being escorted away from the parking lot.

"I hate to bring this up after the conversation earlier, but there's another rumor floating around. Supposedly a former deckhand is claiming that she quit because Michael came on to her. I think she even gave a statement to the police," Maggie said. "I'm sorry."

"No, don't be," Quinn said. "We need to know everything, true or not, so we can be ready to address it if it comes up in the media."

Jonah was just so sick of it all. He closed his eyes and leaned his head back on the seat and pleaded with the universe or whoever was in charge up there for Kira to be returned to them safe and soon. He longed to put his family back together and return to his quiet, semi-secluded life. He couldn't shake the feeling that if he could only find his sister, their mother would pull through—like she subconsciously knew that she could only come out of her coma if she didn't have to face the pain of losing another child.

The girls continued talking about leads and rumors. If only they could hear the screaming that was going on inside his head. He took a deep breath with his eyes still closed, until he felt calmer. They all needed to remain strong and in control for each other. If one of them lost it, the whole tapestry would unravel like it almost had with Michael earlier.

He watched the scenery fly by outside his window. Much of the distance between Makawao and Kihei was nothing but thick groves of trees lining the Haleakala highway, and all he could think of was Kira. Was she really in there or had his gut led him astray? What if he was wrong and they'd lost all this time focusing on the jungle?

He pushed away the thought that if someone had abducted her, she'd likely be dead by now. Instead, he concentrated on Lani's voice as she talked about the cost of a helicopter and how useful it would be, covering much more ground than those on foot could do. She said she'd called every helicopter tour owner on the island but so far no one had been willing to volunteer theirs.

"Ten thousand dollars just to put it up there," she said.

"Helen would pay it, wouldn't she?" Maggie asked.

"Absolutely. She'd do anything to get back in favor with Mom and Dad," Jonah muttered under his breath. "Especially Mom."

They all fell into an uncomfortable silence.

As they arrived in Kihei, traffic was snarled, and pedestrians crowded the corners as they waited to cross. All around him the world continued, and it felt surreal as he watched conversations happening, joggers running, children being herded across the walkways.

Jonah felt the truck slow down then take a turn.

"We're here, guys," Quinn said.

She pulled into the driveway and shut the ignition off in front of a small but well-cared-for house. Jonah whistled at the majestic banyan tree in their yard. He'd known Maria and her family for a while, through Quinn, but this was his first time seeing their home.

He climbed out of the truck and prepared to do something he never liked to do.

Ask for help.

Maria met them at the door and beckoned them inside, embracing them all, then leading them straight through the house and out the back door. She explained that her father was on the beach and it would be a good place to talk.

"Great idea," Quinn said, taking the lead to the beach path with Maria behind her and the rest of them in a line with her son, Pali, at the back, toting his surfboard.

"Where's Alani?" Quinn asked.

"She's at a friend's house," Maria said. "Instead of a lemonade stand, they've decided to start a lei stand. They're having a sleepover to brainstorm and prepare their inventory. Then she's got to set up a marketing page and an online storefront. I tell you, that girl's life is busier than mine these days."

"Sounds like she has your entrepreneurial spirit," Quinn said. "Please give her my love."

"I will," said Maria. "And I am so sorry about Kira. And your mom. Your poor family can't seem to catch a stretch of good luck."

Jonah raised his eyebrows. Quite the contrary, his family owned the trademark on bad luck.

"Any good news yet?" Maria asked.

"Well, Mom's holding her own. Stable but no improvements," Jonah said. "Nothing on Kira yet but we're not giving up. There's a team searching the jungle as we speak." He waited to bring up the issue of the SAR team calling off their efforts after this evening. No sense in explaining it twice since her father would need to hear it too.

"Good," she replied. "Don't lose faith. I've been meditating and I feel like she's still with us. Somewhere."

"Thank you, Maria," Quinn said. "That means a lot."

"By the way, Jonah, I met Kim," Maria said with a smile. "She's not only beautiful, but she's smart as a whip. You need to hold on to that one."

That was a sentiment Jonah heard a lot these days, which, to him, was an uninvited indication that people knew too much about his personal life.

"Oh? How did you meet Kim?" he asked, suddenly going stiffer around the shoulders.

"I took a lunch basket up to the hospital for your dad. He was busy caring for your mom, so they sent Kim out to the waiting room. She's lovely. Really."

Jonah heard Pali chuckle behind him. He turned and scowled but had to look up to meet Pali's eyes. The boy had grown at least a good five inches since Jonah had last seen him. Was he seventeen now? Or maybe it was eighteen. Either way, he was turning into quite a handsome guy and looked strong to boot. It was no wonder that Liam and Pali's father, Jaime, sometimes had to flip a coin to see who got to use him on the construction site for the day. It was always nice to have a strong back available in that line of work. Not to mention that Pali was getting to learn the craft from the best.

"What are you laughing at?" Jonah teased. "Let's hear about *your* love life."

Pali's grin disappeared. "Nope. Not going to get Mama started."

Maria shook her head. "This boy goes through girls faster than I can learn their names. I don't even try any longer. But I know one thing, opportunities are like sunrises—if you wait too long, you might miss them. And

I'm talking to you, Jonah. Pali has plenty of time to be young and free."

Everyone but Jonah laughed as they stepped onto the beach.

He spotted the Kupuna right away. The old man sat in a sun-bleached bamboo chair, facing out at the ocean. There were three others with him.

"Who else is here?" Jonah asked.

"Helen," Quinn admitted. "I didn't want to scare you off by telling you I called her. I explained everything and she agreed to come and thought it'd be a good idea to ask Carmen to attend. Then Liam suggested that Auntie Wang join, as she has a lot of clout in the community and can probably help too."

Jonah felt blindsided. He wasn't prepared to ask a panel of elders for help. Hell, he didn't like asking anyone and he wouldn't have, if it weren't a life-or-death matter.

He could handle his grandmother, but he barely knew her old friend, Carmen, other than the fact that she'd been partially responsible for sending Quinn to the mainland to be raised by her best friend.

Together, Helen and Carmen had irreversibly changed the course of his sister's life—of his life. He wasn't one to hold grudges, but he'd also never forget the part she'd played in his family's tragedy.

"Jonah, I can feel you cringing from here," Lani whispered. "Think of it like this… we haven't found Kira on our own and we're losing what little help we've had. If our efforts on the ground aren't working, we have to pivot and do something else."

Pali bounded ahead and kissed his grandfather on the top of his balding head, then plopped down to sit on the sand between his feet.

Helen greeted the rest of them with a wave, then

pointed to the only empty chair and told Maria she'd saved her seat.

Jonah went straight to Maria's father and held his hand out. Even without sight, the old man knew it was there and took it, holding it warmly before he shook and released. Jonah went to his grandmother and kissed her cheek, bringing a huge smile to her face. He moved to Auntie Wang and did the same, knowing the traditional greeting would make her happy.

Carmen stood and kissed each of the girls on both sides of their faces. But when she turned to him, Jonah pretended to be interested in a seagull.

Though the woman was around the same age as his mother, she looked much older. Years of guilt, Jonah surmised, though he also knew that even at her age, she still lived the life of a rancher, and the elements could be harsh on the body.

He tried to imagine her as a young woman, finding a child she knew to be lost by a family she held a grudge against, then hiding that child until she could conspire with his grandmother. All the while, the child's mother—*his mother*—was putting herself through a guilt-inflicted hell over leaving her children alone on a boat.

Jonah still felt bitterness. He swallowed it back and reminded himself that Carmen was also the one who had finally brought an end to the mystery when Quinn returned to the island searching for answers. If Carmen hadn't gone to his grandmother and insisted that they come clean, the family might never have known what happened to the little sister he'd known as Nama, who'd disappeared off their boat during a freak squall. They might never have had the opportunity to develop a relationship with her now, as Quinn.

"It's good to see you all," Carmen said, then sat back

down on her beach chair, her eyes suddenly on her feet. She dug them into the sand childishly, as if the million grains could cover her sins.

Auntie Wang smiled widely at the group and waved them all to sit, then popped her umbrella open, blocking the sun from her body.

"That's my cue," Pali said. "I'm going to catch a wave or two."

He bounded up, grabbed his surfboard, and headed out to the water.

"Yes, take a seat and let's get started," Kupuna said, finally speaking to quiet the greetings. "Auntie Wang, Helen, and Carmen, thank you for coming. It feels good to catch up on family business."

Jonah wondered what the elder council had discussed prior to their arrival but pushed it aside. He wanted to make this quick and easy so he could get back to Makawao and the business of finding his sister. And as much as they needed help, it also felt wrong to go on a spiritual quest when he was more of a fan of action that yielded visible results.

But he had enough Hawaiian blood in him to know to be respectful. He joined the girls sitting on the bench in front of the elders.

The Kupuna spoke first, looking toward Jonah.

"Your grandmother has filled me in on your family's latest challenges and your sister's disappearance. I'd like to hear from you just how you think I can help."

Jonah cleared his throat. It was hard to talk about. Actually, he'd never had to speak of the family curse himself, thinking that if he avoided the topic on his tongue, he could keep it at bay. He'd never decided if he believed in curses or not, but the shame left behind by the actions of his great-grandfather still burned.

Speaking of it was painful, but he'd do what he must.

"As you probably know, one of our ancestors wronged Carmen's family. It's believed that because of that act, Maui elders put a curse on our family."

The Kupuna nodded solemnly. "I know. It was a battle over land ownership that ended in vengeance."

"Then you also know that my grandmother eventually brought the families to a truce, and it was thought that the curse was broken."

"Some stains never fade," the Kupuna said.

"That's the problem," Lani broke in. "The new generation has caught wind of the old stories, and the community has turned against us. We need support and resources to find my sister, but backing has trickled to nearly nothing. It's like we're living the old *sins of the father* proverb."

"Carmen and her family have forgiven the Rochas, so why can't the people of Maui do the same? This grudge goes against the spirit of aloha, in my opinion," Maggie said.

Jonah cringed. He wasn't sure how the Kupuna would take Maggie's direct way of speaking. He hoped that the old man remembered Maggie was from the mainland and would grant her a little mercy.

The Kupuna smiled at Maggie like a doting grandfather.

"Maggie, do you know what *'aina'* means?" he asked, his voice low and understanding.

"Land," she replied, impressing Jonah.

"That is correct, in a roundabout way," Kupuna said. "It literally translates to *that which feeds us*. Just think about it like this: to live, you must be fed. Hawaiians have a very deep relationship with our land. To take someone's land is to take away the ability to care for his or her family."

As the old man talked, Jonah listened but followed

his empty gaze and was treated to the view of a surfer taking a wave, then riding it in. Others headed out, paddling frantically as they watched for the next good ride. All of them were oblivious to his family's pain. Unaware that a young woman—a daughter, wife, and pregnant mother of two little boys—had vanished into thin air less than an hour's drive away, leaving behind a trail of agonizing questions.

The Kupuna took a long breath, then continued. "The land gives life and after we die it is the land to which we return. Our ancestors are buried there, and their spirits give us guidance. It's sacred, and to lose any of it unwillingly—even one tiny pebble—is a tragedy unto the very soul of those who have lost it."

"Amends have been made not only toward my family, the Crowes, but also the community," Carmen said. "Helen has become one of Maui's greatest philanthropists. As Maggie said, my family has long ago forgiven theirs."

Jonah noticed his grandmother was unusually quiet. More than anyone in his kinfolk that he knew, she still suffered over past sins the most.

"Just because it is forgiven does not mean it is forgotten," Kupuna said. "However, with the help of other Kupunas, I believe we might be able to turn this around. Let us see if the spirit of Pono can be revived in those who have a grudge against your family."

Or if they're willing to let my sister die out there.

"Thank you, Kupuna," Quinn said, her voice quivering. "We really need to work fast. We need more volunteers: searchers, hikers, divers even."

"Don't worry, child. Here in Maui, we live by *Kōkua aku, kōkua mai.* Tomorrow, things will be different. Tomorrow, we will see change."

"Accept help and help others," Jonah said. He remembered that one from his childhood, though he didn't think the younger generations held much to it any longer.

"*Mahalo*, Kupuna, and everyone else," Jonah thanked them, then stood.

It was time to get back to Makawao. He really didn't hold out much hope that a Hawaiian proverb would turn the tide against his family, but at least they were trying. And at least he could return to the reserve feeling like they'd done everything they could for Kira and the delicate life she held inside her that he was determined to meet.

Chapter Twenty

Helen sipped at the cold drink and wondered why in the world anyone would ever want to add ice to coffee when it was perfectly fine steaming hot even in the high temperatures of Maui. She hid the grimace the sweet drink brought to her face. Carmen had ordered for them and Helen wasn't one to complain.

She wasn't sure what Auntie Wang—Gracie, as she insisted on being called—thought of it because she had the utmost poker face.

"I'd like to understand from the beginning," Gracie said. "Why do you think a curse has followed your family?"

Helen waited as a waitress showed up with their banana bread. She set out each plate in front of them.

After their discussion at the beach was over, Carmen had suggested that Helen join her and Gracie for a coffee and a quick discussion at a local diner. She thought that with their combined knowledge and history of the island, perhaps they could address some of the recent events.

"Jules's great-grandfather Rocha came to Maui to work as an attorney a long time ago, and the story goes that much of the land that is in our family was taken from one of his clients in a deal gone wrong," Helen said. "That client was a part of Carmen's family."

Oh, how she hated speaking the story aloud. When she left this world, she would count it as a blessing that she'd never have to do it again.

"I'm not going to deny it. I hated Helen's family," Carmen said. "The vendetta was started by our elders, but the repercussions trickled all the way down to me. It took a lot of self-realization and examination before I finally buried the hate. I had to acknowledge that holding such a heavy grudge wasn't working for me or my family. Once I recognized that, I knew I had the power to change it."

"The same here," Helen said. "I wanted it to stop with my generation and not touch my children, or their children. I worked hard to make it right."

Gracie looked perplexed as she set her cup down.

"But you've made restitution. So, in that case, the curse should've been broken."

"That's what we thought," Carmen said. "And Helen has done more than make restitution. Not only did she eventually make it right with my family, but she's given much more to the community. Still, bad things seem to continue to happen to her people."

"Like my granddaughter being swept off her parents' boat and lost at sea when she was a child," Helen said. "The curse went after what Jules loved the most: her children."

"I remember when Quinn returned to the island looking for her father. Liam brought her to me," Gracie said. "She's a dear girl."

They were silent for a moment.

"I don't know all the facts," Gracie continued quietly, looking at Helen. "but it would help if you explained to me why when Nama was found, you arranged for her to be hidden away."

Helen almost choked on her coffee. The woman was brazen; she'd give her that. But Gracie Wang was well-respected on Maui for her wisdom and her connections. If she could help in any way, the truth would be worth telling.

Helen leaned forward, sighing loudly.

But before she could start, Carmen broke in.

"I was the one who found Nama on the beach the morning after she'd gone missing from the boat and at first, because of the feud between our families, I was going to just keep her for a few days and let the family suffer a little more."

Helen noted the look of horror that crossed Gracie's face.

Carmen lifted her chin. "Let me be clear that I'm not proud of my actions. But I was young, and years before that I had lost my beloved horse in a barn fire that we were sure was set by someone in the Rocha family. So not only had they stolen valuable land from us, but they'd taken the life of my best friend. I was still bitter and for a long time, I wished I had a way to get back at them."

"Our family didn't set the fire," Helen said. "But I can understand why they would suspect us."

"I knew Nama was Helen's granddaughter. The whole island knew who she was. And I thought my plan was the perfect way to make the Rochas feel a little of the pain I felt when I lost my horse."

Gracie nodded. "The human psyche is complicated."

Helen cleared her throat. "Carmen only kept her a day or two and then called me."

"Why not call the police?" Gracie asked.

"Everyone knew of the feud between our families," Carmen said. "If they found me with Nama in my possession, they would've never believed I'd innocently found her. I didn't want to be accused of kidnapping. I was trying to avoid the media circus and just quietly send her home."

"She called the number on the posters and I picked up," Helen said. "I was already convinced that the curse was the reason Nama had been swept away. When I heard from a Crowe, of all the people, stating that she had my granddaughter, I broke down. Nama had been delivered straight into the arms of the Rocha's worst enemies. You tell me, how in this universe that could happen if not ordained by fate?"

Gracie nodded. "It does seem like improbable odds."

Helen continued. "I was frantic trying to figure out the best way to handle it. In my traumatized thinking, I honestly believed that if Nama was thought lost at sea, and I could still ensure she was safe and healthy, then perhaps sending her away would end our curse once and for all. I wanted to save my daughter any more pain. She had another child. A beloved son. And I knew that she wanted more. Would fate pluck every last one of them from her if I returned Nama? Instead, I could give Nama a good life away from the island that tried to take her while convinced that sacrificing her would save the rest of the family."

Carmen cleared her throat and raised her eyebrows. "That wasn't my line of thinking," she said. "I was barely twenty years old and my thought process wasn't that deep. However, Helen convinced me that somehow, I would be in serious legal trouble for my part in finding Nama and holding on to her like I had. That it could be considered kidnapping. I was afraid, so I recruited Beth, to take the girl to the mainland and help her start a new life."

"But you tried to get her back," Gracie said. "I believe that's what I heard."

Helen nodded. "Yes. After the chaos died down, I came to my senses. But when I tried to convince Beth to bring her back, she went underground and disappeared."

"Then we were forced to stay quiet about it," Carmen said. "Neither of us wanted to go to jail. If we could've gotten Nama back, we would've come forward. Helen hired private investigators and never stopped searching. But neither she nor Beth could ever be found."

"Why didn't you at least let Jules know her child had not died at sea?" Gracie asked. "Give her that much to ease her pain?"

"We thought about it, but we both decided it would be easier for her to grieve Nama's death than to never be able to find her or know for sure that she was okay," Carmen said.

"I honestly thought Nama was lost forever—as good as dead—until Quinn came looking for her family," Helen said. "I got the shock of my life when Carmen came to me and said Nama was back on Maui and didn't know her real identity. We decided it was time for the truth to come out. Years and years of keeping the secret had made both of our lives miserable."

She sat back in the booth, suddenly exhausted. The details were more dramatic and complicated than any movie she'd ever seen or any book she'd read. It was still hard to believe it was her life she was talking about.

Her mistakes.

Gracie looked sympathetic, though Helen didn't know if it was for Jules or for her and Carmen. Hopefully, Jules because Helen knew she didn't deserve anyone's sympathy. She was lucky that Quinn had insisted that forgiveness be granted, or Jules and Noah most likely would've shut her out of their lives forever after finding out what she'd done.

And that would be no less than she deserved.

But she was angry. "And now Jules had a stroke and Kira went missing both in the same day? You can't tell me the curse is not real. I don't care how much the superstition scares people to acknowledge. I've lived it. I'm still paying for the sins of my father, and now my daughter is paying as well," Helen said.

Gracie frowned. "There's got to be something more. Something deeper, probably going back to even before the land issue."

Helen shook her head. "Not that I know of."

"Let me do some digging," Gracie said. "I'm pretty good at what I do and if there's anything else we should know about, I'll find it."

"Then what?" asked Carmen. "How is that going to find Kira or help Jules?"

"I can't promise it will do either, but something has to be done, unless you want your family to keep dodging tragedies for all eternity."

Helen put her head up and closed her eyes. But she didn't pray. She'd done enough of that for decades and it hadn't brought her any relief.

When she opened her eyes again, Gracie was staring at her.

"Just tell me what I need to do to make this stop," Helen said. "Please."

Gracie nodded solemnly. "I'll do my best."

Chapter Twenty-One

Jules felt someone standing over her and realized she was no longer on the boat. It was dark again. Her body was cold and heavy. Cumbersome.

But not wet.

She heard voices coming down around her, first just faintly and then loud enough to understand.

"She's always felt the need to help others," Noah said. "Her family, strangers, and every needy animal that's ever crossed her path. She's the epitome of selflessness. From the day I met her, I knew she was special even though we were both so young."

Jules listened to him talk about her, knowing that he gave her too much credit and held her on too high a pedestal. She wasn't that person. Other than finding him and having their children, her life was a series of mistakes and bad luck.

"Yes, I've heard about your outreach program to those who live on the beaches," Kim said. "It's a wonderful program. But sometimes, Noah, part of the reason that people are altruistic is because they long to heal a wounded part of themselves and don't know how. It's easier for them to focus on helping others than on helping themselves."

"Could be," Noah said. "Jules once told me her father

was so busy making money that he was rarely around, and her mother tried to form her into the perfect daughter, or at least Helen's perception of what a Rocha daughter should be."

Jules tried to remember her childhood, but nothing came. It sounded very sad, if Noah was correctly describing it.

"It's really an unsustainable way to go through life," Kim said. "While it's a good thing to be selfless and giving, at some point she needs to turn that around to herself. Unfortunately, people like her are always living in some sort of crisis mode for the sake of others. It's a huge energy drain and could have led to this physical breakdown, though doctors might refute that opinion."

"Some call it being an empath," Kim continued. "They feel and absorb the emotions of others around them to the detriment of their own psyche."

"I wish I had noticed," Noah said. "Jules tends to bury her own feelings, especially about the past. I thought that she had moved on, so I never encouraged her to go deeper and face things."

"It's not too late. You can help her when she comes out of this," Kim said. "Show her it's okay to be vulnerable and to focus on her needs, rather than on everyone else's. If she can find her inner strength and take on her own trauma, that's when she can truly be the healing person that she wants to be for everyone else."

Trauma.

That word scared Jules. Had she been living with suppressed trauma? Is that what had brought this on?

The question sent her seeking the black void again. Call it instinct, but she knew she didn't want to explore any deeper what trauma meant to her. She shut down the idea and focused on silence. She wanted the dark. She wanted to find the euphoria she'd briefly tasted, then lost.

She felt something touch her hand.

"Jules, are you in there?"

Her heart shifted. It was Noah. Her anchor to the present.

"If you can hear me, squeeze my hand," he said. "Please, Jules. I know you're struggling but I also know you haven't left me yet. Kim and I are right here, and we aren't going anywhere. You are not alone."

The anguish in his voice cut Jules to the quick and triggered a memory of the last moments she felt alive.

The water. And the storm.

And something more.

Something so terrifying and traumatic that Jules knew that though she couldn't remember what it was, she didn't want to go back there and experience it again.

She needed Noah to keep her here, safely with him. Even though her body felt unfamiliar and so broken, her mind was safer with him than wherever it had been before.

The vision of Kira still filled her with a dread she could do nothing about. She could sense that her daughter was hurt and completely depleted. If someone didn't find her soon, it would be too late.

"One squeeze, Jules. You can do it. I need you. The kids need you."

Jules told her brain to connect with her hand. To move it.

Just once, damn it. Let him know you're still here.

With all the effort she had in her, she urged her hand to lift.

"She moved her finger!" Noah exclaimed loudly. "That's my girl, Jules. I knew you could do it."

"Are you sure she did it?" Kim asked. "I didn't see it."

"I'm sure, Kim. No doubt about it. She moved that

finger right there, only a second or two after I asked her to. I'm calling the nurse."

He went to the door but before he did, he squeezed both of her hands and she felt his warmth rush through her.

"You've got this, Jules. We know you're in there and we're going to help you find your way back to us."

Day Five

Chapter Twenty-Two

Jonah tossed and turned, knowing he was dreaming but unable to wake himself. He was back in the desert, and his company was visiting a tiny hamlet surrounded by opium-poppy fields. They'd been there two days and had already built a well and cleaned up a park, trying to make it fit for the children who remained in the crumbling village. Those who were brave enough to still have hope ran around outside as though their world wasn't falling apart.

That was the thing about dreams, you already knew how they'd end, and Jonah fought against the next scenes, the dream within a dream. The little girl showed up out of the alley and approached him for help. Her dark hair and trusting face instantly took him back to another time, on a boat when his dark-haired little sister needed him to protect her from the storm but instead was yanked from his arms and toppled right into the waves.

He'd gone in after her, of course; that was what big brothers did. But the waves separated them quickly and he nearly drowned himself before he was found and pulled back to safety. They couldn't find Nama. They never found her. And he'd been the one who had let her go.

There, in the godforsaken desert of Iraq, Jonah was instantly frozen in fear. Not from the girl—but from the idea of letting her down. She reached out and took his hand, then led him down the alley from which she'd come, straight into a mud-walled shack of sorts.

Jason, and of course Beaker, too—named for his high-pitched voice like one of the Muppets—followed grudgingly. They were always with Jonah, his eyes and ears, protecting him even if they didn't agree with some of his choices.

They stopped in the doorway. The room was so dark he couldn't see anything until his eyes adjusted.

The girl stood there, dressed in layers of unmatched and filthy clothing, her feet bare and dusty. Her hair hadn't been combed in weeks and it had probably been even longer since a washing. He wondered when her last meal had been even as he reached for the candy in his pocket, handing her the last of what he carried.

Not more than four or so years-old, she'd grown up in a warzone and had a sense of which soldiers were safe to approach. She trusted him.

She led him to her mother's bedside. The woman was wet with perspiration. He touched her forehead and felt it burning beneath his hand. A question screamed in his head. Were he and his team responsible? Had she been left to navigate a difficult birth alone because of them?

She didn't have accusing eyes—only wild ones filled with pain.

Staying there was dangerous. The woman was unchaperoned. Half-naked. If her brothers, father, or anyone from the village came and found soldiers there, there would be hell to pay. But Jonah refused to leave her that way, so vulnerable and helpless.

His brothers in arms weren't so sure. It came to a screaming standoff right at her bedside, but Jonah eventually won out and convinced them that helping her was the right thing to do. They'd seen to the woman and the screaming infant at her breast, both of them laying in the middle of a dark circle of blood staining her makeshift bed.

The girl brought a bucket of water and Jonah himself had cleaned the mother, while doing his best to maintain her modesty. He'd also washed off the baby and wrapped it in a clean sweatshirt from his bag. They'd moved fast and then loaded them into the truck to deliver the family of three to the nearest temporary hospital.

The little girl—the one who reminded him so very much of his lost sister—was taking the ride silently, her curious eyes watching the scenery fly by through the open window.

The mother was so weak, and Jonah hoped she'd hold on long enough for them to get her the help she needed. She handed him her baby to hold, then gathered the blanket around herself and huddled against her daughter. She was shaking with cold, even though it was hotter than Hades in the desert.

His team had given him a new nickname for the occasion. He was no longer Maui Boy.

Now they called him *Baby Daddy*.

Jonah didn't think it was funny, but that was what they did to survive. They made humor out of tragedy—and it worked. For a little while, anyway.

Suddenly, there was an explosive sound and Jonah jerked upright, expecting to see the charred remains of his brothers in arms.

But he was back in Maui.

Thank God.

Someone unzipped the front of Jonah's tent in one fluid motion, and a blast of sunlight cut through the dimness that was his cave.

Derek squatted and peeked in.

"Up and at 'em, lazy bones. You need to see this for yourself," he said.

Jonah rubbed his eyes, relieved to be away from the hot desert and bloodcurdling memories again. But then he remembered why he was sleeping in a pup tent at the Makawao Reserve. He felt the return of helplessness that he'd had when they'd returned from Kihei the night before and it had been too dark to go back in. He could only imagine how afraid Kira was, out there all alone. It had taken him hours of tossing and turning, until completely depleted, and he'd finally fallen into a hard sleep.

He looked out over where Derek pointed.

"Wait. I thought they pulled SAR. What are you doing here?" he mumbled.

"This is on my own time. I can't let you go hammering through that jungle without some brains behind you, now can I? Brought a few members of my crew, too. The ones who could get away from work."

Jonah looked away so that Derek wouldn't see the rush of gratitude that threatened to drown him. It was going to be a long day, but at least he wouldn't be doing it alone like he'd been prepared to do.

"What's all that noise?" he mumbled.

"It's called Aloha spirit, and it's just what we need. You were sleeping like the dead. Get your ass out here on the double," Derek said, then stood and walked away.

Jonah got to his knees and rummaged through his backpack for a clean shirt.

Derek didn't know the ironic timing associated with his words.

His friend had interrupted the dream just at the point of impact. The finale. The horrific reenactment of the worst moment in his life. Jonah would never get over the guilt because while he had survived the explosion of the truck, his buddies hadn't.

If not for his insistence to follow the girl and his order that they get her family medical attention, his unit wouldn't have been trailed after leaving the hospital and he wouldn't have to be punished with constant memories that crept in as nightmares, haunting his conscience.

He stumbled out of the tent and stood, looking over at their basecamp.

He saw people. Lots of people.

Damn, Derek was right, He'd slept hard. Not surprising, considering how long he'd been going on next to no shut-eye. He always knew that at some point, he was going to hit a wall.

Vehicles filled the lot and he saw a small group of people carrying climbing equipment to rappel the cliffs. Liam was among them, as were his brothers.

He raised his hand and waved. Jonah waved back.

Jonah saw another guy carrying an oxygen tank, obviously ready to suit up and explore the waterfall pools.

There was Rita, the manager of the market in town, pulling out a box of wrapped food.

And the owner of the Haiku Yoga Studio was handing out flyers to everyone who approached the scene. Jonah knew they would show Kira's smiling face.

He couldn't believe it. It appeared that whatever the Kupuna had done, it had worked. It almost seemed as though the family curse had been broken after all.

Jonah wished his mother was there to see it. She'd always tried to distance herself from her family name, but today she would have been proud.

Lani spotted him and waved him over, a huge smile across her face. She pointed at a chair near her and when Jonah squinted against the sun, he could make out who it was.

Michael stood there looking at a map in his hands, and in a chair beside him sat Maria's father, the Kihei Kupuna.

There was no doubt by the strong lift of his chin and the way he held on to his cane beside his chair that the old man was in charge.

Emotion flooded through him.

It meant Kira still had a chance.

It wasn't too late.

Derek was talking to the Kupuna, explaining what they'd done thus far in the search.

"We've hit every possible corner of our grid. The problem is that it's so damn dense in there that it's easy to overlook any evidence. She could be unconscious just beyond a screen of brambles and might get missed."

The Kupuna nodded. "That is what I was thinking. And that's why we need more manpower. You take the grid again. This time with twice the number of searchers fanned out."

"Morning," Jonah said. "Thank you, Kupuna, for coming."

"It is my honor."

Derek rubbed his hands through his hair. "I see what you're saying, Kupuna. But my team got pulled. Our manpower is minimal. Other than myself, we don't even have any skilled hikers for the deep ravines. There are masses of fallen timber down there. It's too dangerous for the average person."

Kupuna nodded solemnly. "I know. But that was *your* manpower. Mine is on its way. You and Kira's husband will lead them."

Jonah looked at Derek over the Kupuna's head, and Derek smiled like the Cheshire cat.

"And you," Kupuna directed his gaze toward Jonah. "You will be at basecamp to coordinate everything."

"With all due respect, Kupuna, I'd like to be boots on the ground in the jungle, searching for my sister. Her husband can be in charge at basecamp."

"I know you would, but we need leaders at the frontline and based on your experience, that's you," he replied.

Jonah didn't want to argue even though he doubted the Kupuna's faith in him. Whenever he was put in charge—of Nama and, later, his brothers in arms—he lost people. The old man didn't understand. Jonah wasn't a leader. In fact, he might be the ill omen.

Before he could form a rebuttal, Maggie and her friend approached with Woodrow on their heels. The dog's tongue was out and his tail was wagging; he probably assumed he was about to go on the best walk ever since this had all started.

"Jonah, you remember Juniper," she said, gesturing at the young woman.

He nodded. "Thanks for coming."

Juniper was a tiny shot of dynamite with blue tips at the ends of her hair, a ring in her nose, and what looked to be a tattoo of a mermaid twisting up her bicep. She was pretty unforgettable, though. Instead of the tie-dyed clothes he remembered her wearing the last few times he'd seen her, this time she was dressed in khakis, a camo shirt, and heavy boots with Wonder Woman socks sticking out the tops.

"This is Derek, our lead on search and rescue," Jonah said, introducing the two.

Derek tipped his head to her and Juniper smiled, then immediately launched into what she'd obviously been dying to say.

"Jonah, that friend of Kira's from the coffee shop in Makawao went to the print shop and paid for a thousand flyers. I've got them being delivered to Haiku, Kihei, and Lahaina. They're also posting them on signs all up and down Hana highway. I know it's a longshot, but you never know who may have seen her that day then went back to their own area."

"You're right. Thanks for working on that, Juniper," he said. "We also need to send some fliers to be hung in Paia, and all over the high-traffic areas in Kahului."

"Already in the works," Juniper said.

What Jonah didn't say aloud was, this was a crucial task in case some of the doubters were right and Kira really wasn't in the reserve.

Maggie stepped in. "Jonah, Liam called and said he found a helicopter, but they want a thousand dollars an hour," she said.

Jonah whistled through his teeth. "Jeez."

"That's actually cheap, man," Derek said. "What about your grandmother?"

Even Derek knew Jonah was related to money. It embarrassed him.

The Kupuna shook his head before Jonah could answer. "No. It's important that we do not use money from the Rocha estate. Or the Monroe's."

"Even if it could save Kira's life?" Jonah asked. He didn't want to insult the Kupuna, but time was of the essence. They needed that copter.

Kupuna nodded. "Trust me, Jonah. If there really is a grievance the 'aina is harboring toward your family, your money will only bring bad luck."

Jonah didn't agree, but he needed the Kupuna and his resources, so he'd do what the man said.

"I started an online donation campaign," Maggie said. "So far, it's not up to much, but hopefully it will take off."

"Where's Lani?" he asked.

"She's over there helping set up our new basecamp," Maggie answered. "Michael is guiding the move."

Jonah looked to see a group of people, including Lani and Michael, carrying boxes and folding chairs into a new covered tent. It was a good one, made like a real room with plastic windows and a door. He saw a fan being carried in and next to the tent, a generator waiting to be used. Someone else carried a wooden tripod and a bigger terrain map than what they'd been using.

"Kupuna," he started, "I don't even know what to say. This is amazing. There must be fifty people here."

The old man nodded, his expression impassive. "*Ka lā hiki ola*. It is the dawning of a *new* day. Soon there will be more here. Word is making its way around. The people of the island are joining together so that your family might be reunited again."

Jonah wanted to believe him.

Chapter Twenty-Three

For the first time since that tragic day on the boat when Jules had lost Nama to the tumbling waves, she felt brave. The dream, or memory, or whatever it was, had rocked her to her core. The deep, intense mourning for her little daughter as she'd looked out to sea, searching for her, had filled her again.

But this time, she discovered that she had the power to choose where to put her energy, and that was into fighting through this place where she had lost control in order to fight for her daughter who was in danger right now.

Nama was no longer lost. She had not suffered and drowned alone out there, her body ravaged by the elements. Fate had sent her on a detour, but then their paths had crossed again when Nama returned to them as a grown woman named Quinn.

Jules logically knew all of this, but her psyche had refused to stop searching, causing the grief to return again and again. The pain she'd carried, the constant yearning for that lost little girl, the guilt at leaving her on the boat…she couldn't do it anymore.

It was done.

Nama's face began to fade in her mind, and then the image brightened until it became Kira's young, eager smile. Always ready to please. To help. And to offer encouragement.

Then Kira as an adult.

Determined. Driven.

But sad.

Even ravaged.

She knew something in the deepest depths of her soul.

Kira needed her now more than Nama ever had.

The intuition filled her with terror.

She saw her daughter again, this time in a different position, propping herself on a rock, her attention on her leg. Jules concentrated as hard as she could.

Let me see more, Kira.

Feel me.

Jules tried hard. So, so hard to reach Kira.

The narrow view widened, but slowly.

There were trees.

And a ravine.

Suddenly Jules was tumbling, head over heels. She could feel the jarring pain as her body was pounded against rough terrain, fighting gravity.

She felt herself jerk. She lay quietly, glad the falling was done.

Then heard the rushing noise of water.

An ocean.

No, not like waves.

More like pressure. A roar she'd heard many times.

A waterfall.

And Kira again.

A cry of immense pain and desperation coming from her, barely audible over the sound of the water.

Then the view started to get smaller. Then even smaller. She was losing it, though she tried desperately to hold on.

She could no longer see Kira's face.

The water was gone, too. Now all she heard was the drip of her IV and the beep of the hospital machines near her.

It exhausted her and she wanted to fade back away to where there was nothing. She welcomed it again.

Then she heard Noah's voice coming through the fog that settled around her.

"Squeeze my hand, Jules," he urged. "You've already proven you are in there. Do it again. This time, use your whole hand."

He sounded closer than ever.

This was her chance.

If she didn't find a way out of the fog, she'd never be able to get to Kira.

With all her might, she squeezed.

Suddenly an onslaught of activity was set in motion around her.

Noah's face was as familiar to her as her own soul. She thanked the universe that it was the first clear image she saw as she emerged from the powerful suction of the dark void she'd clung to for days. He was crying enough for both of them, the tears raining down his face, his fingers entwined with hers.

"You heard me," he whispered. "I'm so happy you're back."

"*Ho'okahi leo ua lawa*," Kim said, standing over her from the other side of the bed. "As my grandfather used to say, one voice is enough. Never underestimate the strength of your voice, even if it stands alone."

Jules was back, at least in bits and pieces. She tried to speak, to tell them the vision she'd seen of Kira, but her tongue was heavy, and her lips seemed to forget how to form the words. The only thing that came out was a low, rasping sound.

There was another bustle of noise, and a woman in a

white coat came through the door. She flipped the overhead light on and Jules flinched.

"I'm Doctor Rozell with the neurology department," she said.

The doctor came close and put her hand on Jules's knee, then peered into her face. Her eyes were kind.

"First of all, you're in the Neurology ICU at Maui Memorial. You've had a stroke and have been in a medically induced coma for nearly five days.

Her tone filled Jules with reassurance. It was the confidence she exuded and the way she connected with eye contact.

"Can you tell me your name?" she asked.

Jules felt a little skip in her train of thought. She knew her name, but it took a second to remember how to make the *j* sound.

"Shh…" No, that wasn't right. She pressed her tongue against the back of her teeth, pushing off. That wasn't right, either. "Jjj," she finally said.

"Good start. You might find that you experience difficulty understanding or speaking correctly for a while. It's called aphasia and it's perfectly normal after a stroke. We'll arrange for you to see a speech therapist to get you back on track, but I don't want you to worry about it right now," the doctor said. "Now let me have a look at you."

The nurse came around to the other side of the bed and Noah stepped down to the end. Kim remained in the chair in the corner of the room.

The doctor took out a pen light and started the examination.

As she worked, she described the kind of stroke that Jules had experienced and the tests that had come afterwards. She talked about complications related to swallowing and mobility.

Jules didn't understand everything she said, but she did recognize that the doctor was trying to get a feel for how much of Jules's brain was still firing and what obvious damage had been done.

Noah rubbed her toes encouragingly.

"Lift this arm and make a fist," the doctor said, pointing at Jules's left arm.

She complied.

But when instructed to do the same with her right, Jules couldn't do it. She could lift her arm to a point, but then it felt too heavy and she dropped it. It was an awkward movement and her arm felt like a foreign appendage, but the doctor assured her that eventually she would regain her strength.

"I'd like to see if you can sit up," the doctor said, waving the nurse around to her side. They pulled her IVs out of the way and adjusted the top of her gown.

Together they guided Jules into a sitting position and swung her legs slowly to the side of the bed to dangle.

Jules immediately felt dizzy and closed her eyes.

"Lay her back down," the doctor said, gently maneuvering her onto the pillow and elevating her legs again.

"What do you think?" Noah asked.

"I think she'll recover," the doctor said. "Mrs. Monroe, you obviously have an extraordinarily strong willpower because five days after your initial stroke, you brought yourself awake. At least for now."

"For now?" Noah asked.

She smiled at Jules. "Sleep will be your best friend for a while. Lots of rest is what your brain needs to regroup and get back to what it used to be."

Jules tried to shake her head no.

She couldn't rest! Kira needed her.

"What can we expect next?" Noah asked.

"Well, I'd like to keep a close watch on her for the

next twenty-four hours before we move her out of the ICU, but if all goes well, we'll have her in a regular room tomorrow."

Jules tried to squeeze Noah's hand again. Tried to send him her urgent thoughts of Kira.

He felt her squeeze, but took it the wrong way.

"That's amazing," Noah said. "When do you think she can go home?"

"Let's not get ahead of ourselves here," she said. "I'm going to put an order in for some more scans to be sure the bleed has stopped and that we're back on solid ground. She'll need to have sessions with a physical therapist to see how she does getting up and around on her own. We'll run a series of tests to see what sort of rehabilitation she's going to need. Then from there, we'll see."

Jules felt her energy seeping away. She tried to fight it.

"Rest, Jules," Noah murmured.

She had no choice and couldn't keep away the fading.

Jules closed her eyes and she was out, taking with her their only tether to Kira.

Chapter Twenty-Four

Jonah reached up and marked through another natural pool on the big map, indicating it was cleared with nothing found. The teams out were reporting back, and their saturation map was beginning to get more and more colored in as each area was searched.

However, with every passing hour, it seemed less likely that they would find Kira. It was up to him to keep the hope alive so that the volunteers would keep coming.

They'd done a press conference earlier in the day.

Maggie had insisted on pumping the story on all the local news channels. She'd done the talking for them. Jonah had towered over her, trying to heed Lani's instructions to not look so intense, but intense was the only way he knew how to be.

Less than an hour later, an old friend that Kira had gone to high school with had shown up, drunk and belligerent. Neither Jonah nor Lani remembered him, but he claimed to have always been in love with Kira and was out for Michael's blood because he was *just sure* the SOB had killed her. The drama, mixed with drunk tears and exclamations of unrequited love, escalated until a few men wrestled him to the ground.

Emotions were heavy and Jonah didn't want anyone

going to jail, so he talked Billy Something-Or-Other into going home, via one of the biggest Haiku guys they had who would ensure he really got here and stayed put until he sobered up.

Now he stood back and stared, studying the multitude of marks on the map. He thought someone had already searched Fong Ridge, but no one had reported it back. So, had it been searched or not? He sat down at his new makeshift desk, opened the laptop loaned to him, and made a note. That area would have to be added to tomorrow's grid just to be sure it had been covered. It was going to be wasting manpower if it had already been searched, but so be it.

They had to be sure.

Liam would do it. He and his brothers had turned out to be their best climbers. Derek even referred to them as rope masters, no less. Not only were they good at it, but they'd also coached others through some tough ascents, making sure everyone was safe despite their different skill levels. They'd worked damn hard before packing it in for the day, and Jonah was so grateful.

The Kupuna had also gone home hours before, taking most of the stragglers with him on his way out. For the majority of the volunteers, there wasn't anything left to do that could be done without daylight.

Jonah turned when he heard running. Lani came bounding in, with Michael behind her.

"We got footage of Kira from the shops next to the post office in Haiku," she said. She was breathless.

Michael paced the small open space in the tent, his expression unreadable.

"Did she look okay? Was she alone?" Jonah asked. He felt adrenaline shoot through him.

"It was grainy, but she looked fine. And yes, she was alone."

"Could you see her feet?"

Lani nodded. "Yep. That wasn't her shoe that was found the other day. She was wearing black runners."

"What about post office footage?"

"They don't have cameras set up right now. It's a project in progress. And they don't remember seeing her. But at least the shop's footage shows her in her car and turning out of the parking lot, heading this direction."

Jonah's head was spinning with this news. It also meant that it was likely that Kira did drive her own car to the reserve, and it wasn't just planted there. He wished so hard that the reserve parking lot had cameras so that they could verify she'd arrived and had indeed gone into the forest.

"Stellar work, Lani. We can count that as good news, knowing that she was alone and on her way here."

"Yes, but now we worry that she might've picked up someone along the way, or someone approached her here in the parking lot."

"Do you really think she'd pick up someone needing a ride?" he asked.

"I don't pick anyone up unless I know them. But Kira has such a bleeding heart, she might've seen someone having trouble with their bicycle or something. And remember, most abductions are not by strangers. It's usually someone in the victim's circle that they know well, or at least an acquaintance."

Jonah thought about drunken Billy. They needed to check him out too. Though if he knew Lani, she already had a background check running on the guy.

"But there was nothing around her car to indicate a struggle," he reminded her. "Her keys were on the tire and her wallet and phone inside. If someone approached her, I think they would have robbed her. The police haven't mentioned picking up any unidentified fingerprints."

"You're right," Lani said. "But just in case, I'm going to put out a post on social media to ask if anyone saw any hitchhikers that day, or recently in the area. Someone could've grabbed her after she locked up the car when she was heading in for the hike. Also, I called Mike, the owner of the bike rental company. I heard the first sunrise riders came down Kokomo and I'm going to find out if they have GoPro footage and what they saw. It can't hurt to find out if there was anyone walking the roads around here that day."

"Great idea," he said.

Lani continued. "Oh, and David barely got anything out of Maui PD but he's trying. They said they don't work with mainland detectives. David had a good question I hadn't thought of. We don't know if Kira's driver's seat was in its usual position or pushed back further for a taller person."

Jonah hated the line of questioning around the possibility that Kira had been abducted. It caused his gut to seize up. So far, there was nothing to indicate any foul play. But despite his strong feeling that she was in the forest, he knew other possibilities existed and needed to be looked into just as intensely.

"Damn it, I should've noticed that before they took her car," he said.

"Well, they wouldn't tell David. And they won't release the car, even though you know they're done with it by now."

"They've still got her phone, too, right?" he asked.

"Yes, but David did get out of them that there was nothing suspicious in her communications that day. Not to Michael or anyone else."

Well, that was one good thing. He was a little surprised there wasn't something said between her and

Michael that raised flags, considering their conversation about the pregnancy. Hopefully that meant she hadn't voluntarily disappeared, though he would've had a hard time ever believing she'd leave her boys.

Lani calmed down. "And I know you don't believe in any of this, but so far two psychics have messaged the page, and both said they see Kira lying in tall grass. I've got two volunteers that are going to drive Piiholo Road and look for tire marks and search any ditches with tall grass. Just in case she left the trail and took that road to try to get back to her car."

Jonah didn't want to comment on that lead. She was right—he didn't believe in psychic powers, but he was getting desperate and if their predictions brought out more volunteers, or sparked interest in covering more ground, then he'd take it.

"Why would she leave the trail and try to come back that way?" he asked instead.

"Some of the hikers told me that they've left the trail before to explore and ended up on ranch lands, so came out and found the road to get them back. It's not uncommon to be lured off-trail and take an alternate route back."

Tomorrow will make six days that Kira has been out there alone. He felt a wave of sadness and sat down in the folding chair.

Lani approached him and patted his back.

"You're doing a good job, big brother."

A lump formed in his throat. "Not good enough."

"Don't even say that, Jonah. You know we're doing everything possible to find her. Don't manifest any negative thoughts out there!"

He nodded. "You're right. And you're doing a hell of a job, too, Lani. I couldn't keep going without you."

Her phone beeped and she looked down at a text message.

"David's checking in," she said. "I'll get him up to date while you rest a bit."

She left him alone and Jonah watched Derek and his small team exit the trailhead. They all looked as tired as he felt.

When his own phone rang, he jumped, startled.

"Hello?"

"Jonah, this is Dad. Mom woke up."

Jonah leaned back in the chair. It felt like the breath was knocked out of him and he couldn't speak. He hung his head, the phone pressed to his ear as his dad talked, telling him what was going on. He knew his dad could probably hear his ragged attempts to hide his crying and kept talking, knowing in that way that a father just does, to keep the words coming.

Chapter Twenty-Five

Helen was flustered and that wasn't usually her nature. However, she'd been at the hospital with her phone turned off and hadn't checked it in a few hours. After all, who would call her? But when she did finally switch it on, she saw that Gracie Wang had called no less than six times.

It had shaken her when she'd called back, and Gracie told her to get down to the coffee shop and meet with her.

Thank goodness for George. She'd called and told him that she'd been gone a long time because Jules had awakened and asked him to take out the little boss and feed her a snack. He had a key because he was the only one who came around routinely and would notice if Helen suddenly went missing or immobile. Not that she wasn't fully capable of getting around fine, but at least George could open the door if he ever suspected she was in peril.

And he was good with Cinder, so was of course the first one she thought of to step in and take care of her. Cinder would probably pout at her tonight for being gone so long, but Gracie had told her it was urgent.

The tone in Gracie's voice sent Helen scurrying across town. It took a few loops before she got a parking space and she struggled to squeeze in between two cars whose owners obviously didn't know how to park, but finally she was climbing out of her Mercedes and on her way to the door.

When she went through, she saw Gracie in a corner booth and Carmen sitting across from her. They looked deep in conversation and something about their expressions made Helen nervous.

"Hello," she said as she approached the table.

"Oh hi, Helen," Gracie said, a big smile spreading across her crinkly face. "Sit, sit. I already ordered you a coffee. I was just telling Carmen how my husband drops in from time to time."

Helen noticed the urgency was gone from Gracie's voice. She hoped she hadn't ordered her some fancy iced thing, but she scooted in beside her and nodded at Carmen.

Carmen gave her a little wave. She was dressed in jeans and a flannel shirt, quite a heavy outfit for the Maui weather but was usual for her. No doubt she'd already been riding that morning and had probably been cleaning stalls or something of the sort. Helen knew she no longer raised cattle on her land but instead focused on offering horseback riding through their trails for a fee. Carmen didn't guide them herself. She had a team of Hawaiian cowboys for that, though she put in her fair share of muscle in maintaining the stables and property.

"Your husband? I thought you were widowed too?" Helen asked.

"I am. But he lets me know he's still around when I need him," Gracie said.

"He leaves her feathers," Carmen said, smiling down into her iced coffee.

"Feathers?" Helen asked. She couldn't help the doubt that crept onto her face.

Gracie nodded. "Yes. Sometimes if I'm dealing with a big decision or I just need to know he's still around, I'll ask him to send me a feather to show I'm on the right path. And I'll find them in the most random places."

"Like?" Helen asked.

Gracie laughed. "I actually found one in a dressing room once. I was trying on a new swimsuit and cover-up that was a little risqué for me, and I wasn't sure if I could pull it off or whether I was too old to try. I was in there for the longest time, debating it. Just when I was about to take the suit off and leave it behind, I saw a feather sitting right on top of my shoe."

"What kind of feather?" Helen asked.

"I'm not sure. It was a tiny white feather. I kept it and put it in my feather jar, of course. I keep that jar on my nightstand and when I feel lonely, I look at it and remember that he's not truly gone. He's around me, and one day we'll be together again."

For the life of her, Helen couldn't think of how to respond to such nonsense. No one was sending feathers from heaven, but Gracie was kind enough to be helping her family for free and Helen wasn't about to insult her.

"That's really nice," she finally offered.

"He also let me know that he approves of me taking a trip this fall," Gracie said, smiling widely. "You two should join me."

Helen wiggled uncomfortably in her seat. She never left Maui. Or at least she hadn't in years. She felt sure too, that either Jules or Kira—when found—might need her.

"How nice for you. Where are you going?" Carmen asked.

"I'm thinking Estes Park, Colorado. In the winter so I can see some snow, of course. They've got nearly a thousand acres surrounded on three sides by the Rocky

Mountain National Park. I read they even offer workshops in ceramics, jewelry, and basket weaving for those who aren't apt to go skiing or ice-skating. You know what? They will even let you volunteer at the park in exchange for room and board with access to the activities. I might find myself in the laundry room there."

Carmen laughed. "I'm sure you can afford to go without doing hard labor, Gracie. I might be interested in joining you—if I can find someone reliable to housesit and take care of my pets, that is."

"Oh, I hope you can. It would be so fun," Gracie said. She looked at Helen and raised her eyebrows. "You know, Helen, it would be good for you to get off the island for a bit too. See some of the world."

Helen felt her neck heating up. She hated awkward situations, though it shouldn't have been that way. It was just that she couldn't remember the last time anyone wanted her company. Surely Gracie was just being polite.

She honestly wished Gracie would get to the reason she'd summoned her to this coffee date. What did she know that could affect the search for Kira?

"I—well—," she said. "We'll see. First we need to get Jules taken care of and get my granddaughter home."

"I understand," Gracie said. "We can discuss it later, after we get some of this behind us."

"Helen, how is Jules?" Carmen asked. "We heard she's awake."

Helen marveled at how fast information flew around the island.

"Yes, I just left there. She's going to be alright. It's just going to take some time," Helen replied, keeping the prognosis more positive than she actually knew it to be. Truth was, all stroke victims were different, and they didn't know what the future would look like for Jules.

"That's great news," Gracie said. "A friend of mine's husband had the same type of stroke and he passed within six hours. Jules is a fighter."

"Do you know what kind of damage was done yet?" Carmen asked.

Helen and Carmen were friends—or at least acquaintances— but she still didn't like the cut-and-dried way that Carmen asked about Jules's condition. It felt... intrusive.

"Well, we don't know a lot about that yet, but she's definitely struggling with her memory and her speech," Helen said.

"Do you know when she'll be discharged?" Carmen asked.

Helen shook her head. "I don't, but I hope they keep her a little longer. So far, she hasn't asked about Kira. If she does and we have to tell her that she still hasn't been found, Noah is afraid she'll relapse and have another stroke."

"Any news on that front?" Gracie asked. "Other than the Kupuna sending in resources?"

"Not yet. What about on your end? Have either of you found out anything?" Helen asked. "Why am I here?"

They were silent. Helen looked from Gracie to Carmen, and back to Gracie.

"Well? What is it?"

It was perfect timing for the waitress to come by with Helen's coffee, which thank goodness, was just a normal cup of black Kona.

"Cream or sugar?" the girl asked.

"Neither, thank you." Helen took a small sip and nearly closed her eyes in ecstasy at the deep, dark taste of the coffee as she waited for Gracie to spill her guts. It was obvious that something big was on her mind. It had only been a few days since they'd met at Maria's house, so Helen couldn't imagine she'd found out a lot.

Carmen spoke first. "Gracie is somewhat of a historian expert and does a lot of digging around in genealogy."

"Yes, I know that," Helen said. "You've obviously found something, Gracie, so spit it out. I don't need you to cushion anything for me. I'm no wilting flower in case you haven't noticed."

Gracie smiled at her in that sweet, polite way she had. A manner that Helen wouldn't be able to accomplish with a decade of classes at the best finishing school. It just wasn't in her to be that saccharine.

"Yes, I've done some research and I've been quite lucky with going down the right paths of information. Sometimes I get more dead ends than anything but for some reason, this time around, it feels like every door opened to another, more important than the last. As though fate were going on ahead of me to make it easier for me to find what I needed."

"I don't understand," Helen said. "Can you just speak plainly?"

Gracie looked surprised at Helen's tone of voice.

"I'm sorry," said Helen. "I've got a lot going on. I just wish you'd cut to the chase."

Carmen looked sympathetic.

"Don't worry about it," Gracie said, clearly dismayed that Helen didn't share her thirst for the discovery. "That's just some background I wanted you to know before I told you what I found."

Helen sat back against the seat, pledging to keep her sharp tongue to herself. These ladies didn't have to help her do anything, so she needed to exercise some patience with them.

"Eventually, my research led me to talk to an old friend of mine, Charley. He's a Hawaiian historian in his own right and somewhat of an archaeologist. Retired now, but still sharp enough to remember facts in a surprisingly detailed way. He also sits on several Hawaiian preservation boards."

"And how does that relate to my family?" Helen asked.

"Well, to be honest, I went to visit him because your husband's name came up in a lawsuit that he was a witness to."

"What kind of lawsuit?" Helen wasn't that surprised. Her husband had defended tons of people before his death. He'd been a workaholic of the most serious kind.

"It was a case where a contractor had been accused of mining the sand dunes that two historic *heiau* temples were built on near Wailuku town."

"What do you mean mining them? Did he own the property?" Helen asked.

"The contractor owned the property next to the historic ruins," Carmen said. "But he knew he could sell the sand to resorts and make some extra money."

"They stopped the contractor before he could deplete the dunes completely and Charley was called in to assess the damage. He said two magnificent walls were built high on a dune that surrounded other smaller dunes and protected the town from the winds coming off the ocean. The excavation of the sand had caused the walls to begin to crumble, so old stones were piled all around."

Helen felt a tingle run up her neck.

"Not only that, but the contractor accidentally uncovered a lot of burials and bones," Gracie said, lowering her voice to almost a whisper.

Helen didn't know what to say. She knew that digging up bones, especially in an effort to sell the sand they were buried in, was considered an offense to the Hawaiian people, and could easily result in curses or bad luck. Kupuna bones especially were revered, which those must've been if buried next to a temple.

"So, you think that because my husband defended the contractor, our family would've been cursed?" Helen asked.

"Not necessarily," Gracie said. "If he never touched the sand or the bones himself, I don't see how the curse would have affected him. But the subject had Charley so upset that I feel like there's more to the story."

"Even if this happened so many years ago?" Helen asked.

Carmen and Gracie nodded at the same time.

"Charley said that when the restoration teams came, they claimed that many of the stones from the wall they needed to rebuild had come from the small beach village Māʻalaea and were missing. Charley was born and raised at the mouth of the ʻIao Stream and he knew the stones were from there. He had to file legal proceedings himself to make sure that no more of them went missing."

Tingles again.

"What year did you say this happened?" Helen asked.

"He said between 1971 and 1972, if his memory can be trusted, and I have every reason to believe it can," said Gracie.

Helen thought back, taking herself to the first years of her marriage.

"Your husband represented the man who desecrated ancient graves, but as far as we know, he wasn't an accomplice, so we aren't sure why the bad luck would have attached itself to your family."

"There's probably another connection," Carmen said. "If we can find it."

Helen felt sick to her stomach, but she knew what had to be done. She saw it clearly. Perhaps she had always known it somehow in her gut. "We won't have to look far. I think I know exactly what that connection is," she said. "And it'll take some work, but I know just where to go."

Day Six

Chapter Twenty-Six

Jonah held his hands up until everyone was silent. His sisters stood with him, with Maggie alongside as well. They all felt a new urgency now that his mom had awakened. They had to find Kira. There was no other option.

Behind him, Liam and Colby were busy setting up a generator so that the headquarters tent could have some moving air running through it.

Portable fans sat outside the tent, waiting to be hooked up.

Comforts that they'd made it through so far without. Jonah appreciated it, but he didn't need them now, either. He would accept it for the others.

"Good morning," he called out over the volunteers.

Some nodded. Others held their hydro flasks up in a coffee salute. Most wore jeans and long sleeve shirts, while some wore camo. A few sported raincoats or windbreakers, though most of the crew went without.

There was a lot of buzz going on and Jonah scrutinized faces, looking for guilt. He'd gotten it in his head many times during a search, that if someone had taken Kira, they could now be part of the rescue efforts. A sick, twisted way of being involved in their own crime.

Jonah couldn't shake the feeling that in his exhausted state, his mind was playing tricks on him, but just when it started to do that, his heart would lead him true, telling him to concentrate on the search.

The jungle. Kira had to be in the jungle.

Like he'd said all along.

He tried to push off the latest rumor he'd just over-heard about Michael, too. Jonah wasn't going to give it legs. He wasn't surprised that Michael was a suspect in his wife's disappearance or that people would be coming out of the woodwork with stories; some of them true and others just a grab at attention.

Michael had been on his mind that morning, too. He was still at the Maui Police Department, going through only God knows what, just to clear his name. The detective had taken him up on his offer to take a lie detector test.

To Jonah that meant that either Michael was as innocent as he claimed, or he was arrogant enough to believe he could pass the test whether he was guilty or not. Jonah had heard that some people could. Sociopaths and the like. It was a test based on emotion, after all. Or at least that's what he'd always believed.

The results weren't going to be immediate and even if they were, he knew they wouldn't be shared, with the police so tight-lipped about the investigation. That said, Jonah was sure if officials knew something concrete, they'd stop the search and not let volunteers keep trekking through the jungle.

For now, they had to keep moving on until Kira was found. And with people feeling exhausted both physically and emotionally, this was the time for strong leadership.

He and Michael were tag-teaming it, and it was his turn.

Jonah whistled, two fingers in his mouth for a blood-curdling alert, and finally the crowd quieted down and waited for him to speak. He pushed past the butterflies in his stomach. He'd much rather be *in* the crowd, not at the head of it.

It was rainy and chilly day, and he was surprised to have the turnout they did. The elders around the island had spoken, and the people listened.

"Can I have your attention? I'm Jonah Monroe and if you've been here before, you've seen me in the Ground Zero tent. I think most of you have already put some time into this search for my sister, Kira. Our family would like to thank you. And for all of you who are just showing up, thank you too. It's not an ideal day to be outside. I know it's miserable to trek through a muddy path with cold rain falling on your head. So, the fact that all of you are here for what many of the professionals think is a lost cause is a testament to your Aloha spirit. I'm just blown away to be honest."

He took a deep breath. They were also restoring his faith in people, but he kept that to himself.

"Several of you have already asked me the question on everyone's mind: *How long are you going to keep looking?* This is my answer, once and for all. It's simple. If it were your sister—your Ohana—who was missing, would you ever stop searching?"

He looked at Quinn and Lani standing beside him then back at the crowd listening intently.

"The answer is that we won't stop looking until we bring Kira home. She's our sister. She's a dedicated daughter and a loyal wife. She's a mom of two little boys who need her very much. She's a hardworking businesswoman. She's young and in good shape. There have been people found after being lost for longer, in worse shape than she is, so there's still hope. We need all of you. If you can't physically search, you can help us spread the word. You can follow online leads. Hang flyers. Drive down some of these old roads and search ditches."

He turned and pointed at the table of bottled water and snacks already set up. And the one next to it, lined with clipboards to keep a log of searchers.

"Thank you all for playing a role in this endeavor. It takes many hands to keep it all organized, and you have come through. You're joining us on the ground, providing sustenance, combining information... all the things needed to make us a task force that will bring Kira home."

He paused and felt a lump in his throat.

Maggie noticed and took over.

"We still need you to check in and be allotted to a specific team every time you are ready to go back into the reserve, even if it's your third or fourth time," she said. "Francine and Maria will take your name, time of entry, and then you need to check out with them as soon as you are back here. We don't want to be searching for anyone else out there. Raise your hand if you have a smartphone," she said.

The majority of volunteers raised their hands.

"We're going to try something different today," Jonah found his voice and continued. "Since the search for Kira started, we've been keeping up with all the covered areas by word of mouth and marking our paper map."

"Not everyone has reported back either," Derek said. As usual, his friend stood beside him, leaving his own responsibilities behind as he committed to help find Kira.

"Right now," Jonah said, holding up his phone, "I want all of you to download this hiking app onto your phones and mark the coordinates of where you've been, and then send it to the email address that is listed on all the posters. That will ensure that everyone is queued into what ground has already been covered. Using this method, we'll be able to search more area faster, and expand into places we haven't been yet. You can stop by the check-in table if you need help using the app."

He looked at Derek. "Care to add anything?" "We're starting evening missions," he said, "but they will be small, to stay safe and we'll use these crews to fill in the small blanks in the saturation map at the end of the day. If you're on one, bring your flashlight and extra batteries, bug spray and a space blanket, just in case. We need some small drones to check areas too thick to navigate. We'll also have chem lights for the night team. If you've been approved for the night team, we'll see you at 1800."

"That reminds me," Jonah said. "A lot of ground has been covered but we have a lot more to go. I'd like to recruit some fresh eyes to go back over all the main trails and the numerous offshoots. There's always the possibility that we missed her."

"I agree. New hikers will be put together to focus on more of the main gulches and streams," Derek said. "We already have a team that has rappelled the Far East ravines and is planning to hit some cliffs tomorrow and hopefully make it down the few hundred feet to a particular stream bed we are interested in."

Lani stepped up. "We need someone to lead a group down the mountain bike trail, preferably someone intimately familiar with it. See me after this if that's you. Also, please go to the FIND KIRA Facebook page and share it. We need to get her photo out there as far and wide as we can."

"We also need someone with a truck to pick up a group of six volunteer hikers from H-Town. They'll be ready in an hour," a young woman yelled out.

"Anyone with a truck that can go after this meeting?"

Lani asked, scanning the crowd.

"I'll go," a man said from the back.

"Thank you. All of you with trucks have been so helpful. And that's all I have," she said, then looked at Maggie and nodded.

Maggie took a pace forward.

"Hi all. I'm Maggie Dalton and a close friend of the family. Most of you have seen me helping in the main tent too. Tomorrow morning before anyone else goes in, we have a group of hunters bringing their dogs for a search. The leader will be my friend, Red Hill. He's a Maui native and knows this reserve like the back of his hand and can also pinpoint where most of the wild hogs linger."

Jonah swallowed hard. There was always the possibility that Kira had run up on a mama hog with a litter. The wild hogs had tusks that they'd not hesitate to use to impale a threat if they thought their young were under attack. If that was what happened, the dogs would lead the hunters there immediately. The Maui Search and Rescue had used their dogs and found nothing, but hunters' dogs were a different story.

A man in the crowd raised his camouflaged hat. "I have a question."

Jonah pointed at him. "Go."

"Where's Kira's husband? Shouldn't he be here in this rain, too? It's his wife who's supposedly lost in there."

Jonah knew what his dad would do. Michael was family. And he was innocent until proven guilty. He needed their support.

"He's busy investigating another lead. And he's not the family spokesperson, that's why. We decided on day one that as Kira's husband, he's under the spotlight. Not to mention that he's emotional and just as damn worried as we are. But we aren't going to let the public pick apart every word he might say to make him look guilty. That's not a productive use of anyone's time."

The man didn't look pleased with the answer. There wasn't much Jonah could do to clear Michael, other than produce Kira. Until then, his brother-in-law was going to have to keep a stiff upper lip and not let anyone goad him into saying something stupid.

He saw a friend of Kira's and nodded hello. She stepped forward.

"I just wanted to tell you all that Kira and I have gone hiking together before and left both of our phones in the car. Intentionally. To completely unplug during our hike. So, for those of you who are saying that sounds fishy, it isn't. Some people just do that."

Jonah wasn't going to articulate how irresponsible it was for anyone to go into a jungle without a phone. He'd take it as good news that someone knew for certain that it was a possibility Kira had left her phone behind on purpose.

"Thanks for that intel," he said. "We need to know anything we can that will help us decide how to move forward. Anyone else have anything to add?"

Camo hat guy shook his head and mumbled something.

"That's it. We're done. I have to fill in some spots on the map and check some emails. If you're going in with the night crew, please see Derek. Mahalo to you all," Jonah said, thanking them before he turned away.

The crowd dispersed and he set to work once more.

Chapter Twenty-Seven

Jules stared at the ceiling and listened as the blood pressure machine began to beep again. She felt the cuff tighten and her arm being squeezed far too tightly.

Her energy was sapped after a day of trying to get them to talk about Kira.

They continued to push off her attempts to convey her vision and the stroke had left her unable to make much sense.

She'd been moved out of the ICU. She now shared a room with another patient—a woman who was hospitalized for observation after having a series of transient ischemic attacks. They called it a TIA, which basically consisted of temporary symptoms that could be warning signs of a stroke. The nurse explained that they don't usually cause permanent damage, and many call them mini strokes, but technically they aren't.

However, despite her energy and obvious lack of weakness, her roommate was convinced she was in critical condition. With her husband quietly sitting in the chair opposite her bed, she'd spent the morning calling what must've been everyone in her contact list to tell them she was dying of a stroke. While she talked, the husband kept the television blasting the news channel until Helen noticed Jules flinching at the noise.

"Sensory overload," Helen said. Then she'd gone over and had a semi-polite talk with both of them. Now the woman was texting instead of calling, and the television was muted with captions at the bottom of the screen.

Jules was relieved. The noise and activity around her, even when not loud to anyone else, was deafening inside her brain. She longed to go home and be in her own bedroom with the shades closed. It seemed like every two minutes someone was bursting through the door to bring her medication, take her blood pressure, or mark something on her chart.

It was overwhelming.

She rested, telling herself to reserve her energy until Noah returned so she could once again try to talk about Kira and her dire situation. She watched the IV drip, one bag full of fluids and the other holding anticoagulant. The dingy wall around the window needed to be painted. It was cracked and peeling and could be depressing if she let it bother her.

She actually felt she was heading in the right direction and toward recovery. But she also knew that feeling of security could change instantly. It was purely miraculous that she'd found enough strength to get herself into a sitting position, and it gave her a slight feeling of victory. It had taken a technique of rocking back and forth a few times before she could roll upward, but she'd done it and would count it as a win.

Her mother had come over and helped her swing her legs over the side of the bed to sit on the edge, feet dangling just inches above the floor. At first, she'd been light-headed and nauseous, but thankfully that had passed.

As she sat there, her mother kept her arm around her for stability.

"How long?" Jules asked again, relieved that those

words came out as intended. She was having trouble with pronunciations and remembering simple words. She kept things short—her attempts at long sentences had been total failures. Her voice was also soft and weak for now, but at least she could speak again.

"Three minutes," replied Helen, gazing at her phone screen. They were going for six minutes sitting upright, and just halfway there already felt like an hour.

"K.. Kee," she just could not say Kira's name and she was so frustrated.

"Shh," Helen said. "Rest."

Jules wanted to lie back down.

She was also having some trouble remembering things. Like the afternoon of the stroke. She recalled putting Gemma down for a nap and Noah leaving for errands.

And then, nothing.

Noah had tried to fill in the blanks as well as he could, but it was exhausting for her to think about. The future was particularly overwhelming.

All she had was the here and now. And her worry about Kira. That's all she could handle. In a way, the thought of her condition being permanent was tempting, as she wasn't too feebleminded to know that a woman of her age most certainly had a lot of emotional baggage lurking in the suddenly dark corners of her brain.

What if she could walk away from it all once and for all? Just leave it behind in her pre-stroke life as she strived to navigate her life after-stroke?

It sounded heavenly.

However, that meant she'd lose precious memories too.

Complications. Why was the world so full of them?

After a round of exams, Helen had sent Noah home for a shower and a few hours of sleep. He hadn't wanted to leave, but Jules insisted and promised him she wouldn't slip away again.

He'd stared deeply into her eyes and made her promise again before he agreed to go.

When he left, the room immediately felt cold.

She needed him back. Only he could help her get out what she saw.

"The stroke that killed your father wasn't his first one, you know."

Jules opened her eyes and looked up at Helen.

"You were too young to remember, but he survived a few small strokes and another fairly serious one before the big one. We went through a lot of rehab to get him healthy enough to go back to work, only for it to hit him again the final time."

"Why you say?" Jules felt weak again. Her right side felt strange, as though it wasn't a part of her body.

Her mother noticed and pulled Jules closer to lean into her, her grasp strong and solid.

"Because I know how to help you. If you'll only let me," she said.

Jules had no idea why her mother felt that was even a question. And thinking on it further, Helen seemed very hesitant around her. As though afraid she'd say or do the wrong thing.

There was something missing from Jules's memory— some reason her mother was acting strangely.

"Yyy-yes," she whispered.

Helen looked relieved. Or something. Jules wasn't quite sure.

The exercise made her physically drained and the blank spaces in her recall were wearing out her brain.

Helen helped guide her back onto the pillows and then lifted her legs up, tucking the sheet around them.

Jules could see how much her mother worried for

her in all that she was doing to keep her comfortable. It brought back a sudden memory of a time when Jules was in junior high. She'd come down with strep throat and was missing the world surfing competition on the island.

Her brothers had gone on without her and Jules had been unable to stop the tears. That was until her mother had smothered her with attention—and ice pops—and moved a television into Jules's room so she could comfortably watch the event. She'd even stayed with her, cheering when Jules did, pretending like she cared who won so that Jules wouldn't feel alone in her interest.

Jules had forgotten it. She remembered so many times when her mother was cold and distant. Could she be repressing the other side of Helen? And why was it one of the first recollections to recover?

What meaning did it have?

"Sleep now, my girl," Helen said.

That was the best idea she'd heard all day, and Jules closed her eyes. She'd reserve everything she had for Noah. He would understand her the next time.

Chapter Twenty-Eight

Jonah and Colby watched as the professional canine search team got organized with their lead person, who was going over his own map with them. Their arrival had been a surprise that morning. Lani had worked a miracle of sorts, getting them to fly in from the Big Island and to use Kira as a training case. Even though they were in training, the level of professionalism and gravity with which they were treating the case impressed Jonah.

They'd huddled for an hour with the team, exchanging GPS notes and planning the best route to cover the most ground in a day. Unfortunately, a few more hours were all they could spare then they and their dogs would be flying back home.

The Kupuna had thanked them and put an appeal out for them to come back in a day or so if Kira still hadn't been found.

"It's going to be a muggy one," Red said, mopping his forehead with a white handkerchief as he walked up.

He and his hunting buddies had been knocked off the schedule as first in, but he didn't seem to mind. In his mud-stained pants, checkered shirt, and tall, wet boots, he stood watching and waiting for orders with one of his own dogs at his feet.

"Sorry about your dogs having been set aside," Jonah

said. "But this is a good opportunity to get some that have had a lot of training."

"No worries about that," Red said. "Cooter has sniffed out many a wild hog but never been asked to find a person. Still, you never know. We're fine to wait and see if you need us. Cooter and all the others."

Another small group of men stood around an old truck, their dogs prancing around in the truck bed. The men wore the same sort of clothes. Exact boots.

The trained team was looking good, though. The dogs were young, healthy, and looked eager as hell to get out there and do their job. They were all but dancing in anticipation as their handlers talked.

"Whatdya think?" Red asked from beside him. "You betting their dogs will find her?"

Jonah shrugged. "It won't hurt to try. We just have to keep everyone out until they clear the area. Said they need three hours to cross off all the grids on their list."

He and Lani hadn't told anyone else, but there would also be two cadaver dogs going in with the search canines. It made him physically ill to think of it, but the team leader had insisted.

As soon as they were out, he, Derek, and a few of his top picks were going to go back to Kahakapao Loop for another search. It was almost seven miles long, with tons of thick, towering trees that paralleled a deep ravine.

Jonah was eager to get back out there.

Waiting around made his imagination do crazy things.

He could always go back to the tent, but he'd been in there all night, using his flashlight to mark the map with x's where they'd been and noting places further out than the prospective grid that he wanted searched by air. Lani and Maggie were in there now, busy working through the newest emails and social network comments, looking for any valid leads.

As it stood, many were on the bandwagon that Kira had been kidnapped, but there were a vocal bunch that still believed Michael had done something to her. Some of her coworkers had chimed in to say they thought she'd been unhappy or seemed distant.

Of course, that kind of stuff was going to go around. Most people saw an envy-worthy job working on a boat out on the beautiful sea. They didn't take into account how hard the job was, mentally and physically, every day.

Anyone working a charter and then rushing home to tend to their family wasn't going to be seen smiling all day.

If Kira's coworkers had ever seen her on the beach with her boys, or in the midst of a family dinner, play-fighting over who got the last serving of dessert, they'd have seen some smiles. But at the end of a long workday?

Jonah let out a long overdue sigh. People irritated the hell out of him.

At least most of them. But then he thought of all the volunteers who were donating countless hours, resources, and manpower to find Kira and he had to admit there were good people in the world.

Lani also had someone working on returning phone messages, though likely there were more from psychics and the like, which he felt were a waste of time. He touched the burner phone he had picked up for search-related use. He was waiting on a helicopter pilot to call him back. Their campaign to raise money had finally gained enough to pay for an hour of airtime and he wanted to get them up there as soon as humanly possible.

"Did the Maui canine team pick up anything at all?" Colby asked.

"No," Jonah said. "But this pack might."

Just like everyone else, their local SAR dog teams had found no evidence that his sister had ever set foot in Makawao Reserve.

"I remember a few years ago when that young pregnant woman came up missing," Red said. "It was the talk of the town."

"Charli Scott," Jonah replied.

No one who'd lived on Maui at that time could ever forget the tragedy. Her young face had been plastered all over the news and fliers, and her name was on the tip of everyone's tongue. The search had gone on for a long time before they'd discovered her remains.

Red had a long memory and Jonah prayed he wasn't going to start citing every case of people gone missing on Maui. He didn't think he could stomach it.

"Well—I wasn't—" Colby started to say something but was interrupted by an uproar of laughter from a group of volunteers gathered in the parking lot.

Someone had set up another coffee station and as they waited to be assigned and released into the forest, they congregated and chatted.

Their jovial mood rankled Jonah. Too many days had passed, and people were losing their urgency. Kira was already becoming like a ghost—just one of those victims whose names slowly fades from memory. A statistic.

He didn't expect everyone to feel the same way that he and his family felt, but he also didn't want to witness them going on like there wasn't a young woman lost in the jungle just feet from where they stood, possibly clinging to her last breath.

Jonah saw the dog handlers break up and he shook off his irritation then moved to touch base with the leader before he disappeared into the jungle.

By noon, the professional handlers and their dogs were done and gone with nothing more to show for their search than another discarded shoe, someone's lost cell phone, and a report of a burned-out campfire.

Considering Kira didn't smoke and wouldn't carry a lighter or matches, he doubted it was hers, and that he knew of, she didn't know how to start a fire from scratch, which was the first thing he would teach her once they got her out of there.

It was discouraging.

Shattering, actually.

The hunters had also left. Their dogs needed to be fed and watered, given rest from the hours spent waiting with pent-up excitement that they weren't allowed to run off.

"I've still got my dogs here." Jonah heard a voice and turned to find Red Hill, hat in one hand and Cooter at his side. "We'll go in."

Jonah shook his head. He and Derek had hikers ready to check the next points on his map. They'd already been sitting around all day. Or at least the ones who'd stuck around.

But it was nice of the old man to offer. At least he hadn't gotten tired of waiting and just taken off.

"I don't think so, but thank you. If they couldn't find anything, I really don't want to wear your dogs out for nothing."

"I'd really like to give it a try," Red said.

"And our guys are ready to go in now," Derek added. "I don't know if I can keep them around much longer. If you want a hiking team to go, we need to do it."

Jonah looked from Red to Derek. He was torn.

Red spoke. "I don't care how professional that team is or what they did or didn't find. If your sister is in there, we need to pull out every stop. No one knows these woods like Maui hunting dogs. Give us an hour or two at the most. Then we'll come out and you can send in the hikers."

Jonah considered. Red looked half-lame himself. He was at least seventy-five or older. Lean and bent over. But Jonah had to give it to him, the man had waited around all day to do his part. He desperately wanted to help.

And he was right. What would it hurt? The hikers could wait another hour or two and if they couldn't, then hopefully more would show up in the morning. And how far could the old man go, anyway?

If he was leading the charge, they'd be in and out and Derek could send the hikers right in behind them.

"Fine, but I'm with you. I'm not staying out here," Jonah said. He wouldn't be able to live with himself if the old man got hurt in there. The least he could do was insist to be his partner.

Just in case.

He was going to have to change his plans and depend on Derek to hit Kahakapao Loop again without him.

Red shrugged.

"Follow me and I'll show you the map," Jonah said.

Red walked over and with a few curt commands, most of his dogs quieted and sat. He followed Jonah to the tent. Derek and Colby lagged behind.

Jonah pointed at the map.

"We're here," he said, circling a tiny spot. Of course, Red had probably been in and out of that jungle more times than Jonah could imagine. He knew exactly where they were.

Derek, always an encourager, nodded emphatically.

"This is where we want to focus today." Jonah gestured at an area outside of the first phase of searches. "I feel like if Kira was any closer, the teams would've spotted her along the way."

He looked at Derek for confirmation but got nothing.

"Maybe, maybe not," Red said quietly behind him. "Ever heard that saying you can't see the forest for the trees? I've seen it applied accurately many times throughout my life."

Jonah moved on, showing other trails, waterfalls, and pools that he'd prefer they concentrate on.

When Jonah was done, he turned and faced them.

"Are you done?" Red asked.

"Yes."

Red turned. "Then let's go."

The old man was gone in a flash and Jonah raised his eyebrows at Derek, who simply shrugged in reply. They went after him.

In the parking lot, they saw Red drop his tailgate while the dogs jumped out and began to sniff the pavement in every direction. Then Red went to the cab of the truck and pulled a machete out from behind his seat.

Watching them, Jonah realized that though not part of a professional search team, these dogs weren't amateurs. Red had a handheld monitor, and each dog had a collar with a GPS tracker on it, a precaution in case one went too far or got lost.

One by one they were called back by Red, then led to the trailhead where they disappeared quickly. All except Cooter.

"Don't they need something of Kira's for the scent?" Jonah asked Red.

In the tent, they had a box of worn clothes from the hamper at Kira's home. Lani had retrieved them when she knew the dogs were coming, and Michael had been more than willing to allow it.

"Nope. The other team—the professionals as you called them—took that route. My dogs are doing something different. Just let 'em go and see what they come up with."

Jonah was too tired to argue and too discouraged to ask more questions.

Red and Cooter followed the dogs into the jungle, obviously assuming that Jonah would trail behind like a little duckling.

Which he did.

Once they were deep on the trail, Red let Cooter go with a simple command and the dog rushed off to catch up with his pack. He studied his GPS monitor, then tucked it into his shirt pocket.

"So, we're looking for pigs?" Jonah asked.

"Hogs," Red corrected. "I want to check out a few dens. Hey, remember to talk softly or they'll think you're calling them back."

Jonah cringed. He'd already heard that some people thought Kira had possibly been injured and then could've been jumped by a pack of hogs and eaten. The thought of finding evidence of her clothing, or even her body, in a den made him feel nauseous.

He had to get it out of his head.

"Have you been hunting a long time?" Jonah asked, breaking the quiet of the woods around them.

"Yep. Learned to hunt, fish, and forage for food when I was a kid. My daddy made sure we could all fend for ourselves. With a full garden every year and hunting skills, we rarely had to visit a supermarket."

Jonah knew of a lot of Maui natives who'd grown up like Red. He wasn't one of them, since his dad was so sensitive about taking any life.

The dogs backtracked and zipped around them, one almost knocking Jonah off balance.

"Step to the side when they come around," Red said. "They're a clumsy bunch when overly excited. If they catch a scent, they'll go crazy but if they lose it, they'll circle back to us and start again."

That happened more than a few times until finally the pack stopped moving. Jonah and Red caught up to them at a pool of water that had a small waterfall. To the left they found the dogs gathered around a pile of vegetation, barking like maniacs.

Red called them down. They saw a den underneath.

"Want me to look?" Jonah asked.

"I got it." Red got down on his knees and crawled partway in, then backed out.

"Nothing." He stood and let the dogs go.

"We going to check more?"

"Yep. If I were lost out here at night, I'd find a cave or den to get into and conserve my body heat. I'm hoping your sister would think like that too."

Jonah wasn't so sure but the faster he let Red do his thing, the faster they could move on to the next task. Time was catching up to him and the feeling of hopelessness was right on its tail.

Chapter Twenty-Nine

Jules was awakened suddenly by another dream of Kira. It left her feeling panicked, like she couldn't breathe. It was the same one, but this time she could really hear Kira's cries clearly.

Jules felt sick with worry.

Helen approached the bed and took Jules's hand.

Jules clung to her and squeezed it as hard as she could, which wasn't that hard, but she hoped enough to convey her urgency.

This couldn't wait for Noah.

"K.. Kuh…"

"Kira?" Helen offered.

Jules nodded, widening her eyes as far as she could.

"We'll see Kira soon," Helen offered, then stood, breaking eye contact.

She puttered around the room, neatening up Jules's bedside tray and straightening her covers at the end of the bed. She found a stain on the pillowcase and quietly disappeared into the hall with it, then returned with a fresh one and put it on.

"Nnnooo. Kira," Jules insisted.

Her daughter was in danger. Very imminent danger.

Helen wasn't listening to her. Wasn't understanding.

Jules threw her hand flat on the bed in frustration.

"Now don't get yourself upset, Jules," Helen said. She plumped the pillow and returned it to the bed. "Quinn will be here later this afternoon and maybe Lani. And of course, Noah will be back soon. We couldn't keep him away even if we bolted the front doors. He'd just barrel through it like a bull in a china shop. I've never seen a man so devoted. It's like the two of you are just one person and can't be away—"

"No," Jules said, the only word she could think of to quiet Helen's rambling.

Helen pulled a chair close and sat.

"What is it, Jules?"

"Key. Kruh," Jules sighed with frustration and then tried again. "Keer?"

Noah had talked about menial things that morning, but he hadn't mentioned Kira.

They were avoiding talking about her.

And her dreams were more than that. She knew it. She could feel, deep inside her soul, that her daughter needed help. She needed it *now*.

Helen looked away for a minute, then back at Jules.

"I brought you something. Maybe this will take your mind off of things."

Helen rambled through a big bag on the chair. Jules felt like screaming at her to listen. But listen to what? In her total distress, she couldn't communicate what she wanted to.

Helen returned to Jules's bedside and handed her a small leathered-covered book.

"This will help you," she said.

Jules opened the cover. The pages were blank.

A journal.

"As soon as you are able, you need to write everything down and next to it, put a date and time," Helen said. "I read that it's a very helpful tool for stroke victims who suffer with short-term memory loss."

She unhooked a delicate gold watch from her wrist and transferred it to Jules.

"Here, you can use my watch to record the date and time. You don't need all the noise of a phone right now. All that chirping and beeping can drive a mind crazy. Just keep a record and you won't have to keep asking what just happened or who just visited. It will help you feel less confused."

Jules stared at the watch. How long did Kira have left?

A tear of frustration slid out of her eye and down to her nose, then plopped off of her face onto the pillow.

"Oh, I'm sorry. I'm surprised you remember it. You are more sentimental than I am, Jules. It was for our tenth anniversary, but I'm not so very attached to it," Helen said. "I've only worn it for special occasions. But when I got dressed to come up here, I realized it was time to pass it on to you. I think your father would like that."

Right now, Jules couldn't recall any details about her father. All Jules could think about was Kira.

But Helen had a good point. If Jules couldn't *say* what she wanted to say…

She took the pen and put it to the first page of the journal.

It didn't work.

"Oh, let me," Helen said. She reached over and pulled the cap off it, then put it back in Jules's hand.

Jules hesitated. Could she even do it? Would her mind and her hands cooperate?

Then, closing her eyes, she willed the vision to come back to her.

Please, Kira. Talk to me.

The same vision of Kira holding her head came back to Jules. Then, like a fog lifting off of a dark lake, the parameters of the vision started expanding, showing more of the landscape.

More, Kira. Give me more!

And Kira did.

Jules's eyes flew open and she began to scribble in the journal. She didn't even take the time to try to form a letter. That would take too long.

Even so, it took her a while because suddenly, her brain was firing faster than her clumsy hands could work, but when she finished, she pointed to the terrible sketch she'd done.

"What is it?" Helen said.

"Kk...," Jules pointed at the drawing, then made her pen travel down the embankment she'd sketched, and around a poorly depicted waterfall, to a tall wall of tangly bushes.

"I don't understand," Helen said, staring at the sketch.

Jules painfully and slowly added some small circles to represent berries, then pointed again, thumping her pen against the bushes. She took a deep breath and called out her daughter's name. She pulled that memory from deep within her, then spoke.

"Here. Kira here."

Helen stared into her eyes for a moment, looking a little startled at the clearness with which Jules spoke, then thankfully didn't even try to doubt her prediction. She scrambled for her purse and retrieved her phone and started pecking away.

Chapter Thirty

Mainlanders thought the Maui beaches never got cold at any time. They were right too, as the lowest averages were still in the sixties. Not like the Makawao Reserve, where temperatures could drop a good fifteen to twenty degrees when the sun went down, and dip even lower when it rained. That fact always surprised them and had caught many hikers unaware and breathing on their hands to keep warm if they'd lingered too long on the trails.

Thus far, Jonah hadn't let the thought of hypothermia enter his mind.

Now, as he and Red worked their way up the trail, he couldn't stop thinking of it.

Kira being pregnant released the full brunt of the runaway fear he'd been trying hard to keep at bay. How much stress or cold could a fetus take? And the lack of nutrition?

The panic was building in him. What if they found Kira but it was too late? Or if she survived, but the baby didn't?

He knew his sister. She would never get over something like that.

And they could be on a wild goose chase. His gut was wrong before—why was he trusting it so much now?

But if she wasn't in the reserve, the other possibilities scared the hell out of him even worse.

"Too many people getting lost around here," Red grumbled. "I'm getting too old for this and one day old Cooter won't be around."

Jonah didn't comment. The man had his pride.

They weren't too far off from the base of the search, an area that had been covered multiple times. When they came to where the river and a few fallen trees crossed the main path, they turned left and followed the sound of the dogs down the riverbed.

"We're going to get a helicopter up," Jonah said. He thought if he could talk Red into going back, he could send the man home and get back to his own search before it got dark.

"Going to be hard for them to see her with this dense canopy."

"Yeah, but it's worth a try. Kira would know to find the most open spot she could get to."

They'd been hiking and following the pack for nearly forty-five minutes when suddenly they could hear the whining and barking start back up.

"They've found something," Red said, picking up his pace. He checked the monitor and changed direction to the right. They went another hundred feet or so, and through some really thick trees and brush, they spotted a deep ravine.

Jonah was puzzled. He didn't remember seeing it on the map in the tent, but there were lots of ravines. Too many to recall. It had most likely been checked.

"They're down there?" he asked, looking at the dogs through the brush at the drop-off. He wasn't too surprised. Hogs built their nests close to ravines to hide their litters.

But he couldn't see a thing through the trees and vegetation. He really didn't want to waste any more time, especially what it would take to go down and take a look. A ravine was the opposite of an open area, though he hated to point that out to the old man.

"Cooter, I think—" before he could finish, his phone rang. "Hold on."

When he answered, the call dropped.

It rang again. He answered.

Call drop.

Then a text came through from his grandmother.

Kira is down a steep ridge.

Behind waterfall.

Injured.

The text couldn't have come at a more coincidental time. If it had come an hour earlier, he would've written back and said what ridge and how did she know? The fact that he was standing at the edge of a ridge at that exact moment, thinking of skipping it in favor of finding a more open area to search, or even getting out of there to get to work on the helicopter details, was too surreal.

Another text came.

Your mother said hurry. Urgent.

Jonah inhaled sharply, trying to clear his mind. What the hell?

His first reflex was to call his grandmother, but he hesitated.

He didn't want to screw this up.

Was it really too far out of the realm of possibility that his mother knew something he didn't? Some kind of mother's intuition?

Kira always told him there was no such thing as a coincidence. That everything was connected and happened for a reason. More of her free spirit talk, but this time, he was going to listen.

He opened his eyes and read the text out to Red, who

didn't even reply.

Red dropped to his butt and scooted down the embankment, using small trees as handholds as he went. The man was surprisingly agile for his age. Still, Jonah prayed he didn't get hurt. Getting him out of there would be a hell of a feat.

Jonah followed and quickly discovered it wasn't as easy as Red made it look. He hit a few rocks on the way down and grunted as each encounter with a rock caused pain to travel up his spine.

The descent was much, much deeper than it looked— at least fifteen feet—and Jonah was already thinking of how difficult the going back up was going to be.

Once on the bottom, the dogs yipped and yapped at an even higher decibel.

Red used his machete to clear a path as he went, following their sound.

Jonah offered to take the lead and do the chopping, but Red turned him down.

He got the feeling the man was enjoying himself, or at least feeling purposeful.

The sound of the waterfall reached Jonah before he saw it. A chill ran up his back as he remembered the texts.

"They're behind it," Red said, leading the way around.

When they reached the dogs, they saw the pack had surrounded a large strawberry guava thicket. They had given Cooter the lead and he was reacting the most intensely.

The others panted like maniacs, their tongues nearly reaching the ground as Red gave them the command to back off.

He pointed at a nearby tree and then rubbed off bark about two feet from the ground.

"Look at those marks. A big boar left that with its

tusks."

"Must be a den in here," Jonah said, his attention back to the thicket where he spotted a small tunnel through to the other side.

Red approached it and swung his machete back and forth, making quick work of opening the entrance hole bigger.

"Let me take a look now."

"No, let me this time," Jonah said. His heart pounded with the fear he might come face-to-face with a monster hog, but he worked his way through the thicket and came into a dug-out den with a pile of palm fronds next to the opening. Swallowing his anxiety, he pushed further, and his heart stopped when he spotted a tiny snippet of purple through the green.

He pushed his head and shoulder into the den and looked around. It was probably about two-by-two feet and was dug out pretty well. He could tell by the way vegetation inside was flattened that something had been sleeping there recently. More palm fronds were inside, piled to the side. The piece of purple looked to be a torn slice of material, maybe from a shirt or jacket.

Jonah felt sick.

Suddenly the dogs started up. Jonah could hear Red call them down before he called out to him.

"Jonah, you need to come out here."

"Hold on. Let me investigate a little more." Even though he was terrified at what he might find, he needed to see if there was anything else, other than the stench, mud, and fronds.

It was dark and smelled worse than death. He held his breath as he squinted, examining every corner.

"No—come out now."

Red's voice sounded urgent and now Jonah could visualize a gigantic hog headed his way, coming for whoever had the balls to trespass in its home.

He backed out, still on his hands and knees all the way through the thicket. Sweat poured into his eyes and onto the scratches across his forehead. A pine needle stuck in his palm at an especially painful angle.

"Damn it." He pulled it out and kept going.

When he was all the way out, he stood and wiped his muddy hands on his pants. Then he turned to see what Red was stirred up about.

But only one thing entered his line of sight.

Kira.

Chapter Thirty-One

At first, Jonah didn't believe his eyes and was struck speechless. Kira was on the ground trying to rise up, but crumpled down again. She looked like hell, her hair a rat's nest of tangles, circles under her eyes, and the beginnings of sun poisoning scabbing across her nose and cheeks. And she was eerily gaunt.

He instantly worried not only for her but for the baby.

"Jonah," she said softly. Tears ran down her face.

She held the top of a tall, thick stick and he followed it down to her lower leg. It was black and blue and wrapped against the stick with strips of purple material. Her leg was bent at an odd angle.

Broken. Maybe even shattered.

He still couldn't answer her, but he found his footing and leapt forward until he was there before her, on his knees and crushing her in his arms.

"Damn it, Kira. Damn it, damn it," he said, his voice muffled in her hair.

She sobbed into his shoulder. "I'm sorry. So sorry. Thank you for finding me."

Finally, they separated. He sat back to look at her, taking in the ragged clothes. The purple shirt was ripped off at midsection and she was missing a shoe.

She put a hand to her stomach and he just about lost

it again. He quickly prayed that her baby was okay but getting her out of there was his first priority.

Jonah saw Red sitting on a large rock behind her, the dogs resting at his feet. He picked at his fingernails with a small pocketknife, his expression solemn.

He was letting them have a moment.

"Red found you," he said, nodding toward the old man.

Red looked up and shook his head. "Nope. It was all him. He didn't give up. Your brother is a hero. Now we need to make a plan to get you out of here."

Jonah remembered the text. Maybe his mother was the real hero.

They could talk about that later too.

"I'll call Derek and he'll send an emergency team in with a cot to carry you out," he said.

It felt like a dream, but he gently helped Kira to a sitting position.

The dogs sniffed at her, then lay back down.

Cooter took a spot with his nose at her toes, as though he was claiming his prize.

"Where's Michael?" Kira asked.

"Hold on," Jonah said. He dialed Derek's number, praying the signal would hold up.

"What's up?" Derek answered.

"We got her."

"What's her state?" Derek asked, his voice low.

"Injured but alive. Broken leg." Jonah said, looking at his little sister. "Get a crew down here stat to carry her up."

When an eruption rang out from the other end, Jonah had to hold the phone away from his ear. Derek was in full force shouting out commands, the sound of joy and urgency both mingled in his words.

Finally, he came back on the line. "Give me some

coordinates then do not move from that spot."

Jonah checked his app and rattled off the coordinates. "They'll be here soon. And you asked about Michael. He's probably at basecamp. He's been worried to death."

He realized a lot of people owed his brother-in-law a big apology after suspecting that he'd done something to Kira. Jonah felt a guilt-punch to the gut himself. The poor guy had been through so much.

Red handed Kira his phone. "Here. Call him."

Red patted her on the back and took the canteen from around his neck, giving it to her and telling her to drink up. He dug in his pocket and pulled out peppermint candies and handed them over, then walked away to give her privacy.

Jonah heard her sobs begin again. He went in the other direction to make his next call. When he heard his dad's voice, he broke down into sobs, unable to say anything.

"Jonah? Are you there? It's Kira, isn't it?" Noah said. "Just tell me, is she alive?"

"Yes," Jonah got out, pulling himself together.

"Oh, my God. Thank you, Jesus. Was she in the reserve?"

Jonah nodded, then realized his dad couldn't see him. "Yes. In a ravine. From what I can tell, she's got a broken leg, but she looks like shit and I can't evaluate her. I've already called Derek and he's bringing a team to get her out of here."

Noah was silent for a pause, then cleared his voice.

"Thank you, son. I knew you'd find her."

Tears sprang to Jonah's eyes again. He didn't understand why his dad believed in him so much after all he'd done to let him down over the years.

"I just got back to the hospital. I'll meet you down in the ED," Noah continued.

"We'll be there when we can, but it's going to take

some manpower to get her out. I need to call Lani, but I'll keep you updated."

He made a quick call to Lani and they cried together.

They hung up and he joined Kira and Red.

"I called Michael," she said. "I talked to the boys too. The kids are mad that I took a vacation without them."

They all laughed, a stilted, awkward laugh to ward off the emotion. But Kira's ended in a fit of coughs. When she stopped, she gestured toward the thicket where the den was.

"I've been sleeping in there at night," she said, her voice heavy with tears again. "It was nasty and had spiders, and I was terrified that the hogs would come back to reclaim it."

"That shelter probably kept you alive," Red said. "The den saved you from hypothermia."

"I was still freezing cold. Even with the palm fronds draped over me."

Jonah knelt in front of her. "Kira, what the hell happened?"

"I got lost. Can you believe it? I've been coming here all my life and I just… I got lost."

"But a ravine? Why were you down here in the first place?" Jonah asked.

She rolled her eyes at him, a gesture that felt so familiar he wanted to hug her again.

"The ravine was an accident. I wanted to be alone, to think. I sat down on a log, then I thought I heard something in distress. An animal or something, so I tried to follow the sound. I got turned around, then I panicked and got careless and started running like a maniac. I tripped and tumbled over a rock. With the recent rain, the trail was slippery. Anyway, I somersaulted over the side of the trail and into the ravine, until I reached the bottom. I'm pretty sure I broke my leg. I've tried to climb back up a dozen times. Nearly broke the other one before I gave up."

"You're damn lucky you didn't break your neck,' Jonah said.

"You shouldn't ever step off the trail," Red admonished.

"I know," Kira said. "Then I completely panicked because no one knew where I was, and I didn't have my phone."

"You haven't heard anyone calling out for you?" Red asked. "There've been search parties out here every hour soon after you didn't show up for work."

She nodded. "Yes, I screamed my guts out. Then after the first day, I got weaker and couldn't yell very loud. I guess they couldn't hear me over the sound of the waterfall."

That made sense, but Jonah still wasn't sure how the ravine hadn't been searched. He'd carefully marked every covered spot on the map. If it wasn't touched, he would've seen it.

"I heard someone laying on their car horn at night," she said. "It was faint, but it made me feel like I wasn't the only human on earth."

Jonah smiled.

"It was you, wasn't it?" Kira asked.

He nodded.

"I knew it," she said. "The first day I dragged myself around, trying to find another way up to the trail, but I just couldn't climb with my leg so mangled. I came back so I'd be close to where there might be some tracks from my falling. I ate guava to stay hydrated. I didn't pay attention and before I knew it, I was sunburned pretty badly. Enough to make me sick. So, on day three I was up all night, sweating out a fever. The next day I was completely out of it. I swear, I think I was unconscious part of the day and this will sound crazy, but I heard Mom's voice."

Jonah wasn't about to tell her their mom was in the hospital and had suffered a stroke. At least not until they got Kira out of there and stable.

She paused to get her breath, then continued. "I lay in there, fading in and out, until right before dusk. I wanted to just go to sleep and not wake up, but when I heard Mom telling me to be strong, I crawled out and saw footprints. People had been down here, and I missed them. I just lost it then, and again just about gave up hope. I can't believe I didn't hear them, or they didn't see the den."

"We wouldn't have seen it either if my dogs hadn't sniffed it out. You did a good job of camouflaging it," Red said. "Too good of a job, I guess."

Jonah felt sick at his stomach at the missed opportunity, but also relieved that he hadn't neglected a spot on the map.

He reached over and felt Kira's head. "You're still hot. That's enough talk for now. A fever could mean infection. We need to get you out of here. Where's your other shoe?"

"I don't know. It didn't come down the ravine with me."

He looked at her and shook his head. "Why no phone, Kira?"

She shrugged and he saw her cringe with pain before she replied.

She clutched her thigh. "I told you. I needed to think."

He scowled at her. It wasn't the time, but if he wasn't so damn relieved that she was alive, he'd probably kill her for being so stupid. But on the other hand, now that he knew about her argument with Michael, he could understand her needing to get away.

His gaze wandered to her stomach. It also wasn't the time to talk about the life there, but he said a silent prayer that the baby was alright.

Red held his hands up. "You two can talk about that stuff later. The important thing is getting you out of here."

"They'll be on their way soon," Jonah said. "We'll probably have to use a basket and drag you up. How's the leg feel?"

She grimaced. "I'm not gonna lie. It's bad and I'm scared to death. What if it's gangrene? This is the jungle. It can happen fast."

"Let's not think of that right now," Jonah said, though she was echoing some of the same thoughts he was having. He hadn't seen anything that looked that bad since his last tour. But he needed to finish this out strong and that meant focusing on the positive.

His mom was going to come home and so would Kira.

He had never felt more grateful in his life.

Chapter Thirty-Two

Jules was drained of all emotion except for relief. When Helen got the call telling her that Kira was safe, they had cried together. Tears of relief for Kira's rescue and the fact that the stroke wasn't going to take away the upcoming reunion. Then they cried tears that Jules wasn't entirely sure had anything to do with Kira or the stroke.

Neither of them gave words to it and instead, they stayed quiet until Noah returned and then Helen left them, allowing a private celebration with just the two of them over the fact that their child was safe.

Kira was in recovery now, according to Noah. The details were foggy, but Jules remembered he said something about metal pins and surgery. But as soon as she was alert enough, he'd take Jules over in the wheelchair.

After that, she wanted to go home.

It would be sometime that day, but she was still waiting on her physical therapy team to clear her for discharge.

Noah sat with her on the side of the bed, his arm around her lower back. Kim waited with them, busying herself on her laptop as she sat near the window.

Jules needed to get out of there so she could get back to her normal life. Too many people were depending on her. Including Kira, now.

She opened her journal and turned past the sketch, then read the entries from that morning, reminding herself what had happened thus far. Her language patterns and rules were coming back to her, albeit slowly.

Tues 8am Oatmal. Coffee.

9 am: brain dr Roz. Kep me observ. and PT.

10.30 am: Phy therpist. Pract stand. Walk

Her goal to be out to help Kira had sped her recovery up somewhat, Jules thought. Already that day, she'd proven she could stand up next to the bed and take a few steps with the walker—at least enough to get her to the bathroom at home. She was lucky, miraculously so actually, that she wouldn't have to go straight to rehab from the hospital. It might've been a decision based more on the fact that they were self-insured and couldn't afford in-house rehabilitation, but whatever it was, Jules was grateful.

However, at least her speech was returning. If only she could remember the proper words for things.

"How do you feel?" Kim asked.

Kim had arrived early that morning and Jules found something about her straight-shooting nature very reassuring. She liked knowing exactly what was going on in her body and the doctors tended to gloss over the details too fast for Jules to fully grasp.

"Tired," Jules said. "Home."

She found that sticking to one word at a time, instead of sentences, was easier for her to conquer. And even then, sometimes she came out with the opposite word of what she intended.

"Soon, Jules," Noah said. "Be patient."

"Work? How?" Jules asked. She looked at the journal. It was helping her remember details, but it wouldn't be any good when trying to balance the monthly ledger.

Kim approached the bed. "You can't try to force a

full recovery too quickly. Eventually your brain will relearn how to access the things that you already know. The thalamus, where your stroke occurred, acts like the information center. It takes in what you need to know and decides which part of the brain it should go to in order to be processed."

"Like a gateway?" Noah asked.

Kim nodded. "Yes. Sort of. But it depends on the damage and the brain's ability to heal itself. It could all go back to the way it was pre-stroke. And if not, then your brain will figure out another way to process information, like taking a detour on the interstate to get where you are going. The brain is far more advanced than we even know. It can make a miraculous recovery, but you have to believe in it."

"Lost mmmind," Jules said, sighing as she stared at the ceiling and willed herself not to cry. Her emotions were all over the place. She'd never been moved to tears so easily before.

"You haven't," Noah said.

"I like to believe that our mind and brain are separate entities," Kim said. "Your brain is an organ like your heart. But your mind…it's that endless narrative that goes through your head. Some call it chatter, some consider it their soul. It's invisible and it reflects your train of thoughts, your belief system, and your feelings."

Jules wasn't sure why, but she was too embarrassed to tell them that her internal voice had been suspiciously much more silent than normal since her stroke. Maybe that meant she had indeed lost her mind if what Kim said was true.

"They're making huge strides in the study of neuroplasticity and realizing that the mind can help the brain recover new ways to access information from areas that have been damaged from strokes or brain injuries. It's truly exciting," Kim said.

Jules appreciated her positive attitude but the words she was speaking were much too complicated for her at the moment.

Kim smiled. "I'll be making frequent visits to you at home and I plan to use what I've learned to get you back in shape as quickly as possible. You won't be alone through this."

"That's nice of you, Kim," Noah said. "We really appreciate all you've done for us."

It *was* nice and knowing Kim would be coming around made Jules feel a sense of relief. Kim had only been to their home a few times, as Jonah tended to keep his romantic relationships to himself. He'd never allowed Jules to get to know the few girls he'd dated, though in hindsight, she couldn't actually remember any of them now. So perhaps that was a good thing. But Kim—she was different. Jules could sense how much she cared for Jonah.

She hoped it worked out for them.

Noah helped her settle back against her pillows and lift her legs back onto the bed.

"You. Can't help me," she whispered.

"I won't tell if you won't," he said, winking at her. "And you're not going to need to be so independent for a long time, because I won't be leaving you alone."

"Sometimes. Have to," she said, though she felt nervous even considering being alone in the house again.

"If he has to go out, I'll come over," Kim said. "If none of the girls can, I mean. I'm sure they want to be there for you as much as possible."

Jules smiled at her.

That was the second offer in a matter of minutes. It was evident that Kim wanted to be a part of the family.

Just then, the door swung open and Helen walked in.

Jules smiled.

Helen stopped in her tracks. "Oh, a smile? You've missed me?"

Jules didn't reply but the strange thing was that it was true. She knew that somewhere in her memory bank, under lock and key, were boulders of pain between them. But she also knew now that life and relationships were a gift. And that they could be taken away before anyone was ready.

Helen continued. "And speaking of missing, I have a few visitors for you."

Helen went back into the hall and then Jules saw a wheelchair coming in. It was Jonah, guiding Kira through the doorway in a wheelchair. She looked a fright, too. She was sunburned worse than anyone Jules had ever seen, a large scab covering half of her nose. Her leg stuck straight out in a cast and she was dressed in a hospital gown.

"What are you doing? You must've just come out of recovery," Noah said.

"She wouldn't take no for an answer when she woke up," Jonah said. "Caused such a fit that the nurses helped me get her in the chair."

Quinn and Lani were behind them.

"They were ready to throw her out the window," Lani said. "And I was ready to let them."

"Mom?" Kira finally spoke, her voice breaking.

Jonah pushed her all the way to the bed where Kira grabbed on to her mother's arm. Jules leaned down and embraced her. Lani, Quinn, and Jonah huddled in too.

Noah joined them, his strong arms encircling all of them.

"I'm going to leave you all alone," Kim said, making a quick exit and letting the door close softly behind her.

"No, Kim," Jonah mumbled, his voice muffled with

emotion. "Please stay."

She gave him a look laced with gratitude, then joined Helen, standing to the side.

Noah broke away first and sat at the end of the bed. Slowly all of them except Kira let go and stood back.

Kira looked up and Jules saw the tears staining her face, but through them, her little girl smiled. She looked completely and utterly exhausted.

"I heard you, Mama," Kira said, her words thick in her throat.

"I saw you, Daughter," Jules replied.

They stared at one another and Jules marveled at the magic of the bond between a mother and daughter. She looked over at Helen and knew then that theirs hadn't been as close but that her mother had done the best that she knew how at the time and was trying now to do better.

And that is all one can do. Keep trying to do better.

Jules smiled first at Helen then down at Kira as she lifted the sheet.

Kira beckoned to Jonah. "Lift me," she said.

"No, it might hurt your leg," Quinn said.

"Not likely," Lani said. "She's pumped full of the good stuff and it'll last for at least four hours."

"Get her up there, then," Helen said. "Or she'll find a way to do it herself."

Jonah stepped forward but Noah held a hand up to stop him. "I'll do it." Then gently, as only a loving father could do without causing more pain, he lifted Kira up and settled her in close enough that she lay her head on Jules's shoulder.

Helen and Lani worked together to gently prop a pillow under Kira's casted leg.

Jules heard Kira sigh and felt her daughter relax against her. Soon, as the others talked around them,

Kira's breath settled into a rhythm and she drifted off to sleep.

Finally, Jules was completely back, and she knew that despite the peaceful existence that awaited her when her time on earth was done, for now she was right where she belonged.

Out of the blue and back home.

Epilogue

Six Months Later

Jonah watched all the people around him gathered at the beach. Some were still eating, and others sat back in their chairs, telling stories to one another. They probably should've held the gratitude feast sooner, but his mom had insisted they wait until she could walk and talk as normally as possible.

Looking back, the experience now felt surreal, as though it was a near tragedy for someone else, not his family. They had triumphed and brought his sister home.

As a result of all that had transpired, the community had not only forgiven his elders' past transgressions, but they had proven what the aloha spirit was all about as they'd pushed the usual abilities and limitations of their bodies and spirits toward one common goal... finding Kira.

Jonah thought about all the hikers—both young and old—who had struggled through the paths, up and down into gulches and ravines and through walls of tangled briars, searching every square inch of their assigned grids for someone they had never met.

Then there were the ones who did know Kira. Or knew someone in his family. Through this experience he'd come to realize that they had more friends than he'd known of. Old classmates. Fellow boat owners. Many of the beach dwellers who depended on his parents for a regular meal. Even they somehow found their way up to Makawao, many of them hitching ride after ride to get there, to put their own sweat and tears into the search.

The team of ladies that Frances from the veterinarian clinic had put together had worked long and hard too, keeping a log of who showed up, who went into the forest, and who went elsewhere. Their devotion to the details had ensured that every volunteer was accounted for and every man-hour noted.

Maria and the chef from the inn had added special touches to the donated foods, making sure everyone was fed so no one worked hungry. People were still begging for the secret recipe for her famous cookies. Jonah hoped her kindness brought her a lot more customers.

He'd insisted she not help cater this feast, and he smiled at her across the table as she relaxed without worry of serving or cleaning up.

Others there were the ones who'd pinned flyers with Kira's picture onto telephone poles and boards all over the island, from the upcountry to Kihei and down into the corners of the bustling Lahaina. Visitors to the island had canceled their beach days to help look along downside roads, into ditches, and down other hiking paths at other places.

Even old Red had taken a harrowing slide down a ravine but got back up and went right back to work. He and his group of hunter friends had been so generous, using their connections to get permission to stomp across private lands and ranches, allowing them to check every outbuilding and abandoned vehicle in their path, hoping against hope that though they put every bit of caution into their searches, they wouldn't stumble upon something terrible.

Jonah felt his pride swell in his heart, remembering how they had checked in with him, looking for his guidance and his conviction that Kira was alive to reignite the determination in their own eyes and send them onto their assigned tasks with hope, motivating them and healing their brokenness when faced with yet another day of questions.

He'd dug deep and instead of pushing his memories away from his past, he'd used them to keep the morale and resolve of the troops up, pumping them full of words that would fuel their energy.

Giving them purpose.

In that, he'd found it himself.

He thought of Nama and that dark day so long ago. He'd told his mother he'd watch out for her and then he'd lost her.

The tragedy of losing Quinn as a child wasn't his fault. He knew that now.

As he watched her little family, she looked up and met his eyes.

They stared at one another for a long moment and she smiled.

He saw Nama in there. He finally recognized Quinn for his little sister and relief flooded through him. That little girl he knew was no longer lost at sea.

She was home and he could let it go. He was also learning to let go of his guilt about his comrades in arms too. It was a tragic event, but it was not his fault.

Something had shifted inside him and he was on the road to recovery—and hoped that he would soon leave all the guilt behind and stop trying to punish himself for events in his past.

For the first time, Jonah was excited about the future. He'd keep his job at the inn, but he'd also take the position Derek had offered him with search and rescue, and hopefully once again feel that victory after finding someone who was deemed gone for good.

In between, he planned to treat his relationship with Kim in a way that she deserved. A real, old-fashioned courtship because, truth be told, he was smitten with her.

That was the best description he could find. And an old word like that deserved the experience that should be tied to it. Flowers, candlelight, lying in the truck bed and watching the moonlight dance across the water—yep, all that mushy stuff that he'd never delved into was going to be all for her.

Then one day—not too far away, either—he planned to do the whole get-down-on-one-knee thing and make it official. It was time for him to be good to himself and to accept the gifts that the universe was sending him. It was an amazing feeling and for the first time since that tragic day when he watched Nama slip away from him amidst angry waves, he felt free.

Jules watched the kids playing in the surf, listening to their squeals as the water lapped their ankles and tickled their toes. Gemma was the loudest of all of them, her high-pitched voice carrying over the sounds of the boys and just about everything else.

Liam sat beside her, ever patient as she used her little red spade to cover him with wet sand, at times dumping it over his head.

Noah sat next to Jules, his hand on her thigh. She could feel his contentment. They didn't need conversation. Just to be together was enough, watching over their family.

Her friend Kealoha was across the table from them and had just finished talking about their latest rescue of a few whales in a pod that washed up while Jules was in the hospital. The story had a happily ever after, a relief to Jules who didn't want this day spoiled with any talks of death or illness.

"You've given the people on the island a very valuable lesson, my friend," Kealoha said, leaning over to make eye contact with Jules.

"How so?" Jules asked.

"Because your family has taught them to forgive and not to blame the sins of the father on the next generations," she said.

"We'll see," Noah replied.

Jules smiled at Kealoha, a silent gratitude for the talk they'd had the day before. The wise woman had walked her through some very important therapy sessions. The kind of which only someone with Kealoha's experiences could teach.

She glanced at her youngest daughter. Kira sat in a beach chair in the shallowest part of the surf, her legs propped in another chair as she watched Michael and the boys play in the waves. Even though her leg had healed and she had full mobility again, she still refused to be more than a few feet from them. Jules imagined that the trauma of thinking she might die and never see them again would take a very long time to fade.

However, Kira looked serene, even in her progressed pregnancy. As some mothers tend to do, she glowed. She was a happy mom-to-be.

Jules predicted another boy, as that belly hung as low as she'd ever seen a woman carry, but Kira had a feeling she'd be surprised with her own little girl.

Jules saw a new affection between Michael and Kira now. He was no longer wary about showing his feelings. She'd seen him just moments before, kneeling in front of Kira, his hand on the curve of her belly while he gazed up at her and smiled gently.

The disagreement that had sent Kira into the woods that day had been settled and their commitment to their own little family was evident in the plans they worked out for Kira to take a year off work when she gave birth. That would give her the quality time she craved with her boys while they were still young, as well as provide a good bonding experience with the new baby.

Kira also insisted that Jules's days acting as a full-time babysitter to the grands were over.

They would just have to see about that.

Jules loved her alone time with her grandchildren. When she felt fully recovered from the stroke, they would reevaluate. What her children didn't understand was that their children gave Jules a renewed passion for life.

Kealoha continued. "The natural instinct of some humans is to believe the worst in people. And when that happens the negativity can overcome the truth, and a pack mentality forms. Innocents can quickly find themselves the target of hate and intolerance just because it's hard for people to look past easy accusations and not dig deeper to seek the truth. They would rather have something to be immediately passionate about and sometimes, that passion left unchecked, stirs hate."

Jules was glad she hadn't been a witness to the public outcry against her family.

"I think so many people were convinced that the simplest answer couldn't be true, that Kira was truly just lost. She wasn't taken. She hadn't run away. Everyone wants to believe a bigger story. Something meatier and more dramatic. And that hurt us in the beginning," Noah said. "They stopped wanting to help not so much because of our family name, but because they didn't think Kira was in there."

Jules agreed with that and it made her sad that not everyone believed Jonah's unwavering belief that his sister was in the Makawao Reserve waiting to be rescued. But she couldn't be prouder of him. He'd followed his instincts and it had paid off. The family loyalty she'd worked so hard to instill in her children was so evident in all that he'd done to bring Kira home. She felt her greatest achievement was in the devotion she had built, that showed in everything they did as a family.

Helen cradled Cinder in her arms as she approached the table. She was more nervous than she'd been for as long as she could remember.

"Jules," she said, standing in front of her daughter, "could we take a walk?"

"Of course," Jules replied.

Noah stood up first and held Jules' chair, making sure it didn't move in the sand as she got to her feet.

"Yell if you need me," he said softly. She nodded and smiled at him. Helen didn't miss the affection that passed between them. Noah was happier than she'd ever seen him. His relief at having Jules back made him shine from within.

"Can you watch Cinder?" she asked him.

He looked at the dog in her arms and laughed. "Yes, I'll watch her. I doubt it will take much effort. She's barely moving."

"It's her naptime," Helen said. "She'll be happy just to sit in your lap until I get back."

Helen led the way and Jules got beside her, then they linked arms as they walked a few dozen yards away from the noise behind them.

"It's a wonderful day, isn't it, Mother?"

The physical show of affection, and the tone of nothing but joy moved Helen nearly to tears. And it was one more reason she needed to talk to her daughter.

"I accepted an offer on the property yesterday. I'll move out at the end of next month. I'm only using enough funds to buy my new condo and the rest of the proceeds will go toward the Maui Preservation and Historical Society," she said, the words still feeling as though she were playacting.

Jules turned to look into her eyes. "Are you going to be okay?"

Helen nodded. "Yes. I'm fine, and I'm looking forward to living somewhere new. It will be a new start in a place without memories haunting every corner."

After her talk with Gracie, Helen had put two and two together and realized that the ancient stones that made up her beloved garden wall should've never made their way to Hana. First, she'd paid to have her child's remains relocated to a new place. Once that was complete, the wall was taken down, carefully, stone by stone and supervised by one of Maui's best preservation crews.

Finally, they were taken back to Wailuku where they belonged. It had given her great peace to have been a part in the beginning of a restoration project, adding the stones into another wall around the temple ruins.

"Good. I just want you to be happy," Jules said.

"Why, Jules?"

"Why what?"

Helen stopped and turned to face her.

"Why are you treating me so kindly? Since your stroke, you act like a different person."

"I'm happy to be alive," Jules said. "That being said, I've also lost my fear of death and I know that when the time comes, it's not the end of me. It will be a peaceful and beautiful journey, and I wish that everyone could know what I do. If they did, they would live life differently, I think."

Everything in Helen resisted saying the words, but she knew she had to if she were ever to feel any sort of peace again.

"I thought maybe your stroke made you forget our past together."

Jules sighed, then gave a small smile.

"Mama, I can see the pain in your eyes, and I know what you are talking about. The answer is no, I haven't forgotten. But I've come away from this experience with probably the most important life lesson one could ever have. We all walk through life carrying such great burdens, always struggling to move forward. We don't think we are allowed to lay them down. But it's okay to release ourselves from the sadness and burdens we can't handle. We don't have to hide our pain or react to it. We can acknowledge it, learn from it, then let it go. I wish I had known this for the past thirty years."

Helen didn't know what to say. She hadn't heard her daughter call her anything but *mother* since she'd left home. Now she was *mama* again like when Jules was a child. Could it be that Jules finally forgave her? This time really and truly? And not just buried the resentment, but let go of everything in their past?

"More questions in there, I see," Jules said, then chuckled. "This isn't some temporary thing I'm going through. And I want it for you too."

A lone tear rolled down Helen's face.

"I can never lay my burdens down," she whispered. "This family has seen so much tragedy because of me. And because of our name."

"Mama, sit," Jules said. They faced the ocean, watching the sun begin its descent over the water, the rays casting a pale variety of pinks and reds across the waves. "What if we decided to look at things differently?"

"What do you mean?"

"Instead of considering the worst of our family events as tragedies, perhaps they were miracles."

Helen was confused. "I can't see how that could be true."

"I'll explain it. During my stroke, I had to relive the day that Nama fell off the boat. I lost two children at sea. Just bam—instantly gone. Lost in the tall waves and whipping wind. But have we ever considered or given thanks that one child was recovered immediately? Honestly, it was a miracle that Jonah was found at all. I can't even imagine if I would've had to live without him too."

"I never thought of it that way," Helen said. "It was so traumatic that Nama was still missing. And then, when she was found, I ..."

"Shh," Jules put her finger to her lips. "Don't say it. Please. Never say it again. We know what you did and why you did it. But though I missed the rest of Nama's childhood, another miracle brought Quinn to us as an adult. And what a gift she is, Mama."

Helen agreed. It was clear that Quinn was the missing puzzle piece that made the family feel whole again.

"You're right," she said. "She's a very dear girl."

"Not just that, but how amazing is it that only my son—your firstborn grandson—was spared overseas when everyone around him was killed. By all accounts, Jonah shouldn't have been returned to us from that God-forsaken land. But he was. And for that, I'll never stop counting my blessings."

Helen stared out at the water. *Miracles out of trage-dies. She would've never gotten there on her own. Jules was smarter than Helen had ever been.*

"My change of perception has allowed me to feel completely free for the first time since the day that Nama disappeared," Jules said. "In my imagination, I've put all my burdens in a big sack, thrown it over my shoulder and then traveled to the highest mountain peak on the island. Then I laid my burdens down. It has made me feel light with relief. I've finally surrendered, and the universe agrees with my decision. I've found peace, Mama."

Helen nearly flinched when Jules slid her arm around her shoulders. She wasn't used to anyone touching her anymore and for sure not in kindness.

"We were never meant to carry such heavy burdens. We are here, on this earth, to learn lessons, then move on to the next event. There we try to do better. That's all we are required to do. That's all I want from you now."

"Are you sure?"

Jules laughed. "Well, yes. I mean look over there and tell me if I don't have it all? What more could you add to make my life better?"

Helen looked at their family mingling with all of their friends, old and new, and listened to the laughter that rang out. She couldn't think of a single thing that would make it even more special.

"Actually, there is one thing," Jules said.

"What?" Helen asked, sincerely hoping there was something—anything at all—that Jules would let her do or allow her to provide. It had been so long since her daughter had accepted anything from her.

Jules pulled her to her feet. "I want *you* to live again. You're lonely, and don't tell me all you need is Cinder. I'm glad you have that little dog, but you need more. Now that you are getting out of that dreadful house, I want you to travel a bit."

"Oh, Jules, where would I go?" Helen couldn't imagine.

"I don't know, anywhere off this island. Maybe even take George with you. I think he needs a friend too."

"George?!" Helen was aghast. "My gardener? Have you lost your mind?"

Jules laughed again. "Oh, Mama. Don't look so shocked. Kira has seen the way he looks at you, and we all know you call him for a lot of things you could probably handle just fine by yourself. And now that you aren't going to need his gardening skills, you'd better own up to the fact that you just enjoy him being around. You can consider him a companion."

"Hmmpf. I don't know about any of that nonsense," Helen said. But she really could visualize she and George somewhere. He was such a good and solid person, so caring about her welfare. She wondered just how cold Colorado could get and if George had winter clothes stored away somewhere.

"Okay, now that we have some of that settled and out in the open, let's climb your mountain together."

Jules took Helen's hand and clasped it in hers. "Close your eyes, Mama. Then pack away all your hard stuff into a burlap sack and throw it over your shoulder. I know it's heavy, but I'm right here with you and I'll take a turn when you get tired. Now follow me up this path and when we get to the top, I want you to lay it all down and embrace the last years you have left here with us. I want you to feel lighter. And Mama, I want you to live life like you love it."

Helen closed her eyes.

She would try to make the mental journey. No promises, but if it could make her feel as light as Jules looked, she was willing to give it a shot.

When she opened her eyes again, Jules started pulling her toward the ocean.

"What are you doing?"

Jules laughed. "When is the last time you went for a swim and let the water heal you, Mama?"

"Well. I—"

"Exactly what I thought. Me too. It's time for us to at least get our feet wet. Then next week we'll go in a little deeper. Come on!"

She pulled harder and Helen let herself be tugged along toward the surf. It had been at least a decade since she'd touched the ocean and she was a little bit wary. However, when the water lapped up and reached her feet, she felt the tickle of good memories surrounding her toes.

The ocean used to be her sanctuary so many decades ago.

She had forgotten how warm it could be. And how refreshing.

It made her laugh.

Like, a real spontaneous, straight-from-the-gut laugh.

Why had she stopped allowing herself to enjoy the good things?

Jules laughed with her, and like two young girls, they ran along the beach, letting the tide tease them as it chased them in and out of the water.

Suddenly Jules stopped and pointed out to sea.

"Mama, look!"

Helen followed Jules's gaze and saw what her daughter did. A mother whale and its calf, frolicking together and putting on a show. The sight of them made Jules so happy and her joy was contagious.

Helen had never felt so free.

Her daughter was right about one thing.

They had only one life. And it was time to live it.

By the sea.

From The Author

THE STORY BEHIND THE STORY

Thank you for reading INTO THE BLUE, the third book in my By The Sea trilogy. I hope you have enjoyed reading about the Monroe family and their life on Maui. Kira's story was inspired by a true account of a young woman who indeed did get lost in the Makawao Reserve on Maui, for a total of seventeen days in 2019. At the time, my daughter was on the island without any family, and was around the same age, so I was very shaken when the story broke. For the weeks they searched, I watched for news and prayed constantly that she would be found alive. I found myself completely emotionally invested in her story, and as I tend to do with real life events that affect me, I had to get busy writing my own version of how it would conclude.

As searchers continued to find absolutely no evidence that the young woman declared missing had ever even entered the reserve, much of the public (including those armchair detectives on social network) began to spread their own hypotheses of what they thought had probably happened.

The newscasts of this lost woman went all around the world. With it, rumors ran rampant and suspicions ran deep. Had she run away and faked her disappearance? Had she been kidnapped? Perhaps a crazy Maui vagrant or a protective rancher killed her?

Sadly, because of past similar stories involving missing

women, many people pointed the finger at her boyfriend who was the last to see her. Suddenly everything he'd ever done in his life was under the microscope, his character strung up and maligned in front of the world to see.

While the search continued, he maintained his innocence. He took a lie detector test. He cooperated with authorities. He searched with the crews.

Still, the suspicions of his guilt were thick in every mention of the story.

That wasn't all. Even the woman's family members were scrutinized and had asinine allegations about involvement and motives thrown their way. It was clear to me that in times of distress, humans tend to blindly follow along in packs with a herd mentality.

In the midst of all the clutter, there was still a beautiful young woman missing and a rescue crew made up of hundreds of hikers, climbers, and willing hands who refused to give up. There was also her family, who were committed that they weren't leaving the island without her.

I'll admit, as the weeks went on, I began to lose hope for the young woman to be found alive. I also felt such sadness for the family, her boyfriend, and the community. The mob mentality of first a few, and then thousands of people turning against innocents was like a raging river of anger.

The day that the young woman was found in the jungle, injured, dehydrated, but miraculously alive, was a day that humbled many. All those rumors, accusations, and false information spreading through the community, across the media outlets, and across social network platforms showed just how one small spark can start a raging fire of doubt.

As time went on, her story was scrutinized and more theories about her journey and survival spun out of control. But in the end, it was clear what had brought her through. The courage of the human spirit, along with love for her family, had simply won. And the tenacity of those involved in her rescue kept them going, bonded in their belief that she was out there, and cemented in their resolve to keep looking until they found her.

Ironically, the easiest answer was the truth. Like Kira, she was simply lost after going in for a quiet moment to herself.

Through it all, I learned a valuable lesson for myself. And that is to give people the benefit of the doubt, because despite what we see and hear on a daily basis, there truly is more good than evil in this world. We just have to keep spreading it around so that the light can overcome the dark.

Another Kay Bratt novel called DANCING WITH THE SUN, is a story of a mother and daughter who find themselves lost in more ways than one. Carolyn Brown, the New York Times bestselling author, called it *"A baring-of-the-soul emotional story that leaves you with a heart full of love and hope."* When I wrote DANCING WITH THE SUN, I was suffering from a serious case of empty nest syndrome, a common rite of passage for many, that for me bled into the story line between Sadie, and her daughter Lauren.

If you enjoy sinking into a good series, my TALES OF THE SCAVENGERS DAUGHTERS has reached over a quarter of a million readers, and is still a fan favorite.

A reviewer says this about the first book, which can be read as a standalone story:

"A book that made me smile and cry and laugh out loud. I loved every page and can›t wait to read the rest of the series. The story is of a seemingly uncomplicated man who recycles other people›s rubbish to make a living. Only the deeper you get in the book, the deeper you understand how complex he is. He collects children, who for one reason or another have been discarded by their parents. He doesn›t judge the parents but accepts each girl into his home where his wife and him do all that they can to give them a good life. The author is brilliant in how she shows how life is difficult with little money for luxuries, or even for necessities, but full of love and kindness. The family›s struggles but there always seem to be hope. This is one of those books that the story will remain with me long after the book has ended. A must read."

Again, I appreciate each and every reader. If you enjoyed INTO THE BLUE, I would be very thankful if you would leave a customer review on your preferred platform. Favorable reviews are like gold to authors, and imperative for our books to find visibility in the vast sea of new works out there.

For a complete list of my book titles, including series and reading orders, please find my website https://kay-bratt.com. Also, if you'd like to receive my monthly newsletter you will get news of my just-released books, sales, and lots of fun giveaways just for my readers.

You can sign up here: https://www.subscribepage.com/kaybrattnewsletter, but if you prefer not to sub-scribe, you can also hit the FOLLOW button on my author page to simply be alerted when a new Kay Bratt novel is released.

With gratitude,

Readers Discussion Guide

for

INTO THE BLUE

1. A recent epiphany made me realize that many of the characters in my books have experiences that mirror my own. In this book, there is a strong theme of forgiveness needed between mother and daughter. Helen needed forgiveness from Jules for past transgressions. What was your relationship like with the mother figure in your life, and have you had to ask/give forgiveness?

2. Jules needed to forgive herself for leaving her children alone on the boat so many years before. Is there something in your life that you still feel you need forgiveness for doing? Can you see yourself doing something about it now so that you can find peace?

3. All of his life, Jonah carried the guilt for not being able to save his little sister when they were swept off the boat as children. Is there a guilt you still carry from your past that you need to address and forgive yourself for?

4. Jules was a young woman who resented being pigeon-holed into being a part of a rich family, and that carried over into her life choices. Or, considering her characteristics of kindness and humility, do you think her resentment was more about the wrongs her elders had done before she was born?

5. Do you feel that in some way you have also unfairly "carried the sins of your forefathers", as they say?

6. When Kira came up missing and you found out that she was pregnant, was your first suspicion that she probably disappeared on her own, or that something nefarious had happened to her? Were you satisfied with the conclusion that she was simply lost?

Acknowledgments

To the readers of Kay's Krew, and in my online author/ reader book club, thank you for always being there to support my work. For others out there who have a love of reading, I encourage you to go to my website and find the link to join us in our drama-free corner of the internet. Huge thanks to brain scientist, Jill Bolte Taylor, PHD, author of My Stroke of Insight, for a wonderful resource on strokes. The revelations she learned during her own stroke experience were fascinating and led me to write Jules' story. I will forever hang on to Jill's message that we all have the potential to use the tools of our mind to bypass negativity and find inner peace.

I would like to thank my fantastic editor, Sarah Murphy, for taking on the task of helping me take this story from a chunk of coal to a polished diamond. Together we honed the message that we all need to find forgiveness—for ourselves and for others. Thank you to Alicia Clancy and my team at Lake Union who continue to put this series and my other works out in front of readers. This year I surpassed a huge milestone that without the backing of all of you at Amazon Publishing, could've never happened. So, thank you a million times over, for a million books sold.

Many thanks to Maui Search and Rescue, and other volunteers who over the years have given their time and commitment and put aside their own lives for the benefit of helping to save others. Another thanks to the business owners of helicopter tour companies who have donated their aircrafts, and sometimes even the cost of fuel, many times over in searching for the lost or missing.

Thank you to the people of Maui and I hope that I have portrayed your customs and your land to your approval.

Lastly, I am forever grateful to those in my family who love me, support me, and let me be the crazy dog lady who wears her heart on her sleeve, and then puts it into her writing. I know I am blessed, and I am grateful.

About the Author

Photo © 2013 Eclipse Photography

As a writer, Kay used writing to help her navigate a tumultuous childhood, followed by a decade of abuse as an adult. After working her way through the hard years, Kay emerged a survivor and a pursuer of peace—and finally found the courage to share her stories. She is the author of novels published by Lake Union Publishing and under her own label. Kay writes women's fiction and historical fiction, and her books have fueled many exciting book club discussions and have sold more than a million copies around the world.

Kay's work has been featured in Women's World, Adoption Today Magazine, Southern Writer's Magazine, Shanghaiist, Suzhou Sojourner, Historical Novels Society, Anderson Today, and Bedside Reading. Her books have been recommended on LitChat, BookRiot, Midwest Review, Inside Historical Fiction, Blogcritics, The Shawangunk Journal, and Between the Lines (Atlanta, NPR). Her works have been translated into German, Korean, Chinese, Hungarian, Czech, and Estonian.

As a rescuer, Kay currently focuses her efforts on animal rescue and is the Director of Advocacy for Yorkie Rescue of the Carolinas. As a child advocate, she spent a number of years volunteering in a Chinese orphanage, as well as provided assistance for several nonprofit organizations that support children in China, including An Orphan's Wish (AOW), Pearl River Outreach, and Love Without Boundaries. In the USA, she actively served as a Court Appointed Special Advocate (CASA) for abused and neglected children in Georgia, and spear-headed numerous outreach programs for under-privileged children in the South Carolina area.

As a wanderer, Kay has lived in more than four dozen different homes, on two continents, and in towns and states from coast to coast in the USA. She's traveled to Mexico, Thailand, Malaysia, China, Philippines, Central America, Bahamas, and Australia. Currently she and her soulmate enjoy life in their home on the banks of Lake Hartwell in Georgia, USA.

Kay has been described as southern, spicy, and a little sassy. Social media forces her to overshare and you don't want to miss some of the antics that goes on with her and the Bratt Pack. Keep up with her on her monthly newsletter here: *https://www.subscribepage.com/kay-brattnewsletter*

Or find her on Facebook, Twitter, and Instagram, then buckle up and enjoy the ride.

Made in the USA
Coppell, TX
14 April 2021

53732378R00163